M A Z E M A K E R

MAZEMAKER
MAZEMAKER
MAZEMAKER
MAZEMAKER
MAZEMAKER

CATHERINE DEXTER

MORROW JUNIOR BOOKS / NEW YORK

Printed in the United States of America.
1 2 3 4 5 6 7 8 9 10

Library of Congress Cataloging-in-Publication Data

Dexter, Catherine.
Mazemaker / Catherine Dexter.
p.   cm.
Summary: Playing in a maze, twelve-year-old Winnie is hurled back
in time and marooned on a nineteenth-century estate until she can
solve the maze and return to the present.
ISBN 0-688-07383-2
[1. Time travel—Fiction.   2. Maze puzzles—Fiction.]   I. Title.
PZ7.D5387Maz   1989
[Fic]—dc19   88-32349   CIP   AC

For Anna, Emily, and Amanda,
and for the real William Sparrow

CHAPTER ONE

CHAPTER ONE

CHAPTER ONE

CHAPTER ONE

CHAPTER ONE

CHAPTER ONE

CHAPTER ONE

CHAPTER ONE

In summer the schoolyard near Winnie Brown's house turned into a wilderness, and that was how she liked it best—abandoned, with weeds growing overnight and graffiti spreading as if it wrote itself. The cyclone fence gates inevitably broke, and trash blew around and piled up against the bars on the basement windows of the school. The city didn't have the money to keep up the school grounds during summer, and only an occasional police patrol was available to chase away vandals.

There weren't any really bad vandals, in Winnie's opinion. They didn't set fires or break into the school. What they mainly did was spray-paint.

Whoever it was—and they were never caught—painted the playground and the school walls, anything they could find that was blank. They drew swirls and valentines and cartoon words, like "KA-BAM!" in thick, round letters that grew out of one another. There was a blue Casper the Ghost and a tap-dancing Minnie Mouse. They scrawled their made-up names across the walls: "Spanky" and "Duffy" and "The Wall Masters" and "Ted Paper-cut." The vandals left trash and broken glass around; McDonald's wrappers collected in the fence corners. Winnie and her friend Harry Austin picked up the soft-drink cans and turned them in for the five-cent refund.

Winnie and Harry went over to the schoolyard practically every day. Neither of them was going to day camp until later in the summer, and the schoolyard was the only good place to play in their neighborhood, otherwise a street of big two-family houses with minute yards in front and laundry porches in back. Harry's real name was Horace, but who could call him that? It was the same with Winnie—her real name was Winifred, but the only person who called her that was her stepfather, Lew, and he did it in a half-teasing way. He still didn't know quite what to make of Winnie, and Winnie didn't see any reason to make it easier for him.

Though Winnie was twelve and a half, her mother never let her go to the schoolyard without a flutter of warnings. She was a champion worrier.

☼

2

She had lots of allergies, and this had made her cautious by nature.

"Are there teenagers there?" she would ask.

"Sometimes," Winnie would say, not offering any more information.

"Which teenagers?"

"I don't know their names."

"Well, what kind of kids are they?"

"There's all kinds there," Winnie said on one Monday morning in June. "Black kids, white kids, Spanish kids. Did you know Spanish girls get their ears pierced when they're only babies?" Ear piercing was a hot subject in the Baker household. Winnie's mother said she had to wait till she was fourteen, but Winnie said most eight-year-olds had them pierced already.

"Are they smoking anything?" her mother persisted.

"Not that you can see. Not right out in the open," Winnie said, feeling a little mean. She knew her mother wanted to be reassured, wanted a definite no; but Winnie decided to be strictly truthful. "Guess you won't be getting Daisy's ears pierced," she continued. "She would look so cute, though."

Winnie's mother had just finished feeding Daisy. She flopped the baby over her shoulder and patted her on the back. A loud burp came out, and Daisy threw up a little bit of milk on her mother. Daisy was four weeks old and blotchy. She even had pimples. "That's a good girl," said Mrs. Baker

3

soothingly. She got to her feet. A spare diaper and a cotton blanket fell to the floor. She didn't bother picking them up.

"It's not fair," Winnie complained, "is it, Harry?" Harry, who had been present for many similar battles in the past, stared politely through his glasses and said nothing.

Mrs. Baker continued patting Daisy as she carried her out of the kitchen and into her own tiny room at the back of the house. "Babies are so demanding!" Winnie said in an exasperated voice, as if Harry needed to have this pointed out. Harry kept his neutral expression.

"I'll go to that store on Center Street and get them done myself," Winnie called to her mother around the kitchen corner, though they both knew the jewelry store wouldn't do your ears unless you came with a parent.

"For goodness sake, Win," said her mother. "Let's not have this argument now. I was up all night with Daisy. You two go outside."

It was always the same story these days. Winnie's mother never wanted to have this argument now. Winnie picked up a pencil and began to doodle a maze on the margin of the newspaper. She was in the habit of doodling.

"We'll go over to the schoolyard." Around and around went her pencil, making curves inside of curves, till the point snapped.

"You'll be careful, won't you?"

"Mom! You always say that! Of course we will!"

☀

"All right, then."

Winnie went over to the kitchen counter, shoved some dirty glasses to one side, hitched herself up, and pulled down a bag of potato chips, fastened shut with a clothespin. "Let's take these, Harry," she said, and they went outdoors.

They walked around to the back of the house and sat on two aluminum chairs. The Bakers had a small backyard, but it was nice and private, screened from strangers and neighbors by overgrown hedges. Winnie unclipped the bag of potato chips, scooped out a handful, and passed the bag to Harry. "My mom says I'll get fat if I keep eating these all the time," she said. She looked down at a small roll of flesh that came into existence when she leaned forward. "Look. It's already happening."

Harry wordlessly ate potato chips.

"You'll never get fat," Winnie accused him. Harry was all knobby knees and skinny arms. He was a year younger than Winnie, and sometimes she tried to boss him around. "It's in your genes," she said, repeating what she had read in a health book. There had been three drawings of people: basically thin, basically fat, and basically medium. "If your parents are skinny, you will be. If they're fat, you will be. My mom's a little fat—" She stopped uncomfortably. She didn't know if her father had been fat or thin or medium. He had died when she was three. She had only one picture of him, a blurry snapshot that she kept in a drawer. Her mother had married Lew two years ago. Winnie hadn't wanted to change her last name, so she stayed Winnie Brown while they turned into Mr. and Mrs. Baker.

"Here's Tab," said Harry. Tab was a street cat who had begun hanging around Winnie's yard a while ago. She might have belonged to someone on the block, but this wasn't the sort of neighborhood where people knew all their neighbors, and Winnie didn't know whose cat she was. She was a calico cat, colored white with patches of coal black and honey gold.

Harry reached down and scratched Tab behind her ears. "Only cat I know that's named for a drink," he said. Harry had named her. "Hey, Tab, want to go to school?" Tab put her paws up on Harry's knee and arched her back and meowed. He held the bag of chips up high. "Potato chips aren't good for cats," he said. "Gives you high blood pressure."

"Let's go, Harry," said Winnie.

"Wait. Lemme see how she likes this." He reached into his jeans pocket and pulled out a little stuffed mouse made of purple calico.

"What's that?"

"It's got catnip in it. Drives cats crazy." He tossed it down for Tab, who pounced on it, pawed it over, made tiny, ferocious leaps at it, picked it up, and shook it in her teeth.

"She loves it." Harry shook the last potato-chip crumbs into the palm of his hand and funneled them into his mouth. He crumpled up the waxy

☼

6

bag and tossed it accurately into the trash can behind the garage. He retrieved the catnip mouse, shoved it into his pocket, and they walked up Winnie's street, around the corner, and down Lesser Road toward the Morrissey School. Tab followed them, nosing into occasional clumps of weeds. They cut across Mrs. Karabedian's driveway and trailed along the stockade fence, letting their knuckles bump rhythmically against the upright slats. If Winnie walked fast enough, all the narrow cracks between the slats blurred together and she could see through them into the backyard of the Dunfey Nursing Home. It was wide open, uniformly green, and dotted with metal chairs in pairs. Sometimes very old people were brought out to sit in the sun. Harry's mother had told them that long ago the nursing home had been a grand house, the center of an estate. Winnie could see that it had been a beautiful house once, if she mentally subtracted all the fire escapes and blocked-in porches and the metal awnings curved like closed eyelids over every window.

Beyond the stockade fence sprawled the schoolyard, a ramble of asphalt and metal fences and weeds. In the back corner, where the school property intersected with the yard of the nursing home, an old tree leaned out over the asphalt. The twisted, bare branches had long ago bleached pale in the sun. To Winnie it had always seemed like a ghost. Winnie's mother sent her to a school in another part of the city, and Harry went to yet

☽

7

another school, downtown. His parents had decided they were going to move to the suburbs after next year. The thought of Harry moving made Winnie feel sick to her stomach. She avoided talking about it, and so did Harry.

The school's windows had bars and heavy metal screens on them, and the doors were solid metal; during the school year Winnie had seen people ringing a bell to get in. The school looked like an abandoned fortress, and when no one was there except Winnie and Harry, it seemed that anything could happen. Of course, nothing ever did, despite Winnie's mother's warnings.

"This is a city neighborhood," she would say. "There are oddballs around." Winnie would have liked to encounter a real live oddball, just so she'd know what one looked like. At least it would make her life more interesting. She believed she was getting a serious case of boredom, or maybe something worse than that.

While her mother had been at the hospital having Daisy, she and Lew had been home together, just the two of them, and he had asked her how to do all sorts of things. They had read together at night, and put dishes into the dishwasher, and walked to get ice cream at Bill's to take to her mother. Then, when Winnie visited the hospital, she got to hold the baby, but only as long as she wanted to, which wasn't long.

"You can have her back now," she'd said to her mother after a few seconds.

☼

"I'll take her," Lew had said, and stretched his arms out for his baby daughter. He cradled her in one elbow.

Suddenly Winnie had felt unbearably restless. "Can I go get a Coke?" she had asked. She remembered seeing a soft-drink machine by the nurses' station.

"Sure," Lew said, fishing with his free hand in his pocket for quarters and dimes.

Winnie's mouth fell open. Neither Lew nor her mother had ever said yes to a Coke before, just like that. They always had something to say first about junk food.

"I *can?*" she'd asked.

"Look at the toenails," her mother said to Lew. She hadn't even heard Winnie.

Winnie had jingled the coins and walked jauntily past the other lady's bed and down the hall to the soft-drink machine.

Then her mother came home, and the house turned into a tornado of activity. Lew and her mother scurried here and scurried there, and the baby whimpered in a tiny mewing voice every ten minutes. When Winnie had gone to bed that first night and heard her mother and Lew and the baby below, she had felt the most alone she thought she had ever felt in her life.

"Hey, would you look at that?" said Harry. "Somebody's drawn a maze." A huge oval was outlined on the asphalt in gleaming paint, as if someone had drawn on the ground with silver ink.

☽

9

Narrow paths wound smoothly within the outline. The maze was many yards across and nearly filled the side schoolyard.

"I never saw a life-size maze before," said Winnie. "How do you suppose they did it?" The lines looked too delicate and precise to have been sprayed from a can of paint. Tab snuggled up to Winnie's ankle, meowed, and padded over to the edge of the maze. She appeared to be looking at it, too.

"Let's try it," said Winnie.

Harry shrugged a yes.

"Where does it start?" Winnie asked. They circled the outer border of the maze until they came to the only break. Tab followed at their heels. Winnie held out her arms to the side, as if she were walking on a balance beam, and started along the open path. "I used to be pretty good at these," she said. "The ones in the Sunday paper that you do with a pencil."

Winnie followed the path to the right. It turned after a few feet, and she followed it along a curve until it switched back in the opposite direction. She stepped out. "It's making me dizzy. I'm going to start over," she said. There were different kinds of mazes, she had found out in her "maze phase," as her mother had called it. Some of them were full of false leads and dead ends; some had tricks or games along the way. This time she took a turn to the left, which brought her to a crossroads. She turned to the left again, and around the next bend

☼

she came to another crossing. She turned right and took that path all the way around the circumference of the maze, then stopped again. "My head's going around."

"Let me try." Harry began by going to the left, just as Winnie had on her second try. But then he took a right at the crossroads, and that brought him around the outer edge of the maze. He took a little jog toward the middle, then went around a long curve toward the entrance; then he, too, had to stop. "This isn't one of your beginner mazes," he said, wiping his nose with his arm. His nose didn't need wiping; it was just a comforting habit he had. Winnie had heard Harry's mother tell him a thousand times to use a tissue, and she still didn't realize Harry didn't have a runny nose.

While they both stood there looking at the maze, Tab meowed. Later Winnie remembered that one meow. Then the cat began to pick her way through the maze, tracing around and around the path without a misstep, as if she were tracking a mouse. She paused, her left ear twitched, she put her nose delicately to the ground, and then she continued on the path as it led toward the middle until finally she reached its very center. She made a little pounce. Her body grew lighter, starting from the paws and spreading up. Then she became transparent, and then Tab disappeared.

☽

CHAPTER TWO
CHAPTER TWO
CHAPTER TWO
CHAPTER TWO
CHAPTER TWO
CHAPTER TWO
CHAPTER TWO
CHAPTER TWO

Harry backed a few steps away from the maze, turned, and ran up the incline to the sidewalk. Winnie dashed after him. At the top they stopped and gazed down at the pattern. It gleamed innocently against the dark asphalt.

"The cat—well, it evaporated!" Winnie said, stammering.

"I wouldn't call it evaporating," said Harry after a moment.

"You know what I mean. What did it do then?"

"Disappeared."

"Same thing."

"Not exactly. This is spooky. I'm getting out of here!" Harry's voice creaked, and he took off running up Lesser Road. Winnie scrambled after him, her sneakers jolting on the pavement. She caught up with him just as they got within sight of Winnie's house. Harry stopped abruptly. "It was an optical illusion," he said. His voice sounded steadier.

Winnie squinted and looked up at a tree. "The sun is awfully bright," she agreed. In truth it wasn't, but she felt better saying it was.

"She probably walked into some shade just as the sun hit our eyes," Harry went on.

Winnie nodded. "Optical illusions. They happen all the time." She looked across the street to the mailbox and deliberately made her eyes go blurry. Now it didn't even look like a mailbox. It could be a bright blue humpy visitor from outer space, an alien on thin blue legs. "Like, look at that mailbox. Shut your eyes halfway. It could be anything."

"Right," said Harry. "Well, I'm going home now." Sometimes Harry went off abruptly, just like that.

"I'll bet that cat'll turn up looking for potato chips," Winnie called out to him. Harry turned and waved and then went on up the sidewalk. Winnie blurred her eyes. See? He could be anything—a boy, or an ice-cream man, or a ghost.

She cut around the corner, dashed up her driveway, and went in the back door. Just in time she remembered about the baby taking a nap, and she stuck her foot out behind her to catch the screen door before it slammed.

"Mom?" she called through the kitchen. No answer. She walked slowly down the hall, looking into the study, then the living room. Nobody. "Mom?" For one second she thought her mother had disappeared, too. Then she heard thumps in the basement. Her mother came up the stairs carrying a laundry basket.

"Mom! Want to know something amazing?"

A wail sounded in the distance, from the baby's room behind the kitchen.

"Oh, no," her mother said with a groan. "Maybe she'll go back to sleep. She's been fussy all day." She set the basket down on the dining-room table and picked out handfuls of clean undershirts, fragrant with detergent.

"What is it?"

"I went over to the schoolyard with Harry? Like we said? And there was this maze painted on the ground. And that cat that's been hanging around here came with us, and it walked on the maze—"

"Winnie, please, slow down."

"The cat—walked—on—the—maze, and then it disappeared. Zap. Right before your very eyes. Gone. To nothing."

Winnie's mother stacked Lew's undershirts neatly by the salt and pepper shakers and pulled out a bunch of socks. "What?" she said.

※

14

"Harry and I saw a cat disappear." The baby's cries were growing louder. "It just turned into nothing. One minute it was there, the next minute it was gone."

"You probably scared it away."

"No. It knows us. It was Tab."

"She's definitely awake, isn't she?" Winnie's mother meant Daisy.

"Harry said it was an optical illusion."

"That sounds logical."

"But it was real. The cat evaporated."

"How unusual for a cat. Why don't you pour yourself a glass of lemonade, and one for me, too? I'll bring the baby out to the kitchen." Her mother went to get Daisy.

There were no clean glasses, so Winnie rinsed out two large ones that had milk congealed in the bottoms and around the rims. They didn't come completely clean, but she figured the lemonade would cover up the white lines. She filled each glass with ice cubes and poured all the lemonade into the two glasses. The pitcher was sticky. Winnie put the glasses on the kitchen table and sat down. In a moment her mother came in with Daisy, looking as pert as a robin.

"Here's the lemonade, Mom," said Winnie.

Her mother took a sip. She held the glass up to the light and put it down again, too close to the edge of the table.

"Want to hear about the cat now?"

"Sure." But as Winnie began the retelling, her

☽

mother shifted Daisy from one shoulder to the other and accidentally knocked her glass of lemonade to the floor. Mrs. Baker gave an exasperated cry and jumped up. She handed Daisy to Winnie. "Watch out! Don't step in the broken glass. Look, just take Daisy into the den and watch TV."

Winnie scooped up Daisy and left the room instantly. This was the first time in her life her mother had ever told her *to* watch television.

She propped Daisy in a corner of the sofa and turned on the television set. *The Brady Bunch* was just beginning: the smiling, young mom and her three girls who joined up with the smiling, handsome father and his three boys to form a big stepfamily; and then there was Alice the maid. "It's the story . . . of a man named Brady!" The theme song was as perky as could be. Harry hated it. It was actually a program for younger kids; she had watched it every day when she was little. Winnie started to sing along with the theme song. Then she heard her mother dialing the telephone, so she stopped singing and hastily turned down the sound and strained her ears to listen. "I've had it up to here," her mother was saying, and shut the kitchen door. Winnie turned up the television set again. Daisy slipped sideways, but it didn't seem to bother her any. "That's the wa-a-ay we beca-a-ame the Brady Bunch," sang the chipper children's voices.

By the time the program was over, Daisy had begun to scream again, and Winnie gave her back.

☀

Then she climbed the stairs to her room. On her bottom bookshelf was a pile of paperbacks. That was where she kept her maze books. She picked the thickest one from the stack and stretched out on the floor, wriggling her elbows deeply into the rug. She flipped past the mazes she had done ages ago to a long, dull-looking chapter at the end of the book. It was printed in small, fuzzy type and entitled "Mazes—Historical and Contemporary." She had tried to read it before, but it was so dense, she could never make any sense out of it. The chapter began with the story of the Minotaur in the labyrinth built by Daedalus. Then it described mazes cut in the turf many centuries ago in England, and mazes laid out in stone on the floors of churches. There were Scandinavian mazes laid out on the beach by sailors, and garden mazes with people imprisoned in them. Winnie's favorite part was the description of the Egyptian labyrinths, buried deep in the pyramids, which had men on one level and crocodiles on another. The book didn't make it clear if the crocodiles were alive or mummies; she tried to picture it both ways.

There was nothing about mazes and disappearing. One sentence did catch her eye—something about children "playing May Eve games about a maze, under an indefinite persuasion of something unseen and unknown cooperating with them." Whatever that meant. She thought of the shape of the maze as it lay in the schoolyard. When she closed her eyes, she could see it in purple and green, changing behind her eyelids. She kept pic-

☽

17

turing Tab walking into it and vanishing. She would ask Harry's mother about this, that's what she would do. Mrs. Austin was interested in unusual occurrences, though she had once told Winnie flat out that there was no magic in the world, no real magic—at least none that she had ever heard of.

Winnie put the book back on her shelf and went downstairs.

Lew came home from work earlier than usual. Winnie ran to open the door for him.

"How's everything?" he asked as soon as he came in.

Winnie gave him a hug. He smelled good—like his briefcase of worn leather, and pipe tobacco and newspapers. "Listen, I've got to tell you about something Harry and I saw at the schoolyard."

"Let me say hello to your mother first."

Winnie followed Lew into the kitchen. Her mother, looking frazzled, was pacing up and down with Daisy draped over her shoulder howling.

"She's got a fever," her mother said to Lew. "It came up all of a sudden. It's a hundred and three. We better get her to the doctor's." Daisy's cries were escalating into a higher, frantic gear. It sounded as if she were strangling herself at the peak of each cry. Winnie put her fingers in her ears.

"You have to telephone first," said Winnie's mother. "I've got the number on the bulletin board.

Here, you hold her while I call. And can you get a blanket?"

Lew took Daisy and carried her out of the kitchen, jiggling her on his shoulder, then reappeared with a cotton blanket tossed over the baby's back. Mrs. Baker had dialed the health center and was giving their health-plan number to the nurse. Lew walked up and down with Daisy, patting her on the back, as if that might help.

"We're all set," said Mrs. Baker, hanging up the phone. She took Daisy back. "I'll go on out to the car."

Winnie swallowed. It couldn't be anything serious, it just couldn't. Maybe she should have held Daisy instead of sticking her in the corner of the couch.

Now Lew hustled down the hall, jingling his keys.

"I want to come, too," said Winnie.

"Not this trip. We may have a long wait."

"I don't mind. I can read the old magazines."

"*Not this trip.*" Lew hardly ever raised his voice.

"Okay."

"Be sure to put on the dead bolt. And don't worry. I'll call you as soon as I know how long we're going to be there. Probably no time at all."

Winnie heard the note of mechanical reassurance. She knew he meant the opposite. She stood in the doorway and watched the car pull away from the curb. Lew was driving awfully fast, and neither

☽

he nor her mother waved.

Winnie shut the door and turned the key in the lock. It was suddenly quiet with no baby crying, with everyone gone. She hung the key on its hook by the coat closet and walked slowly down the hall. She couldn't help wondering if things had been like this when she was a baby, if her father had walked around with her when she cried, but she thought she'd probably never find out. Whenever Winnie used to ask anything about her own father, her mother answered in a pinched voice and abruptly changed the subject. Winnie didn't ask those questions anymore.

It was almost too quiet. Winnie stood in the kitchen for a moment, listening carefully. She had stayed by herself plenty of times before, and to tell the truth, it always made her a little uneasy. Nothing was going to happen. But what if something did? Sometimes she teased herself into feeling scared, and then she would switch back to common sense. What if a robber broke in without a sound, or a kidnapper came out of a closet? What if someone broke a window with a rock and climbed in past the jagged points of glass—what if someone knocked at the door?

This had in fact happened once before, and she had practically died of indecision: should she answer it or not? If there was a robber and she didn't come to the door, he would figure it was safe to break in. If she did answer the knock, he would guess she was there alone. Worst of all, she hadn't been able to remember if she had locked the back door. She had been standing where she couldn't be seen, and she had stayed there, frozen, until the knocking finally stopped and she heard footsteps going away. Later she found two pamphlets about saving whales on the floor by the mail slot.

Winnie tiptoed through the kitchen and fastened the back door. She thought it would be quite a while before Lew telephoned, so she had time to call Harry. She dialed his number, and after one ring he answered.

"H'lo?"

"Hi, Harry. It's me." There was an expectant silence. "Guess what? The baby went to the hospital."

"How come?"

"She got a bad fever."

"Is she real sick?"

"I don't know. Lew's going to call me. It's probably nothing."

"Nothing, huh? Say, Tab didn't come back, did she? By any chance? Hold it. My mom's asking me something." Harry's voice went off at an angle: "I don't know. The baby's sick, so they left her at home. Okay." His voice returned. "Hey, Win, are you there by yourself?"

"Yes, but I don't care."

"My mom says do you want to come eat supper with us?"

Did she ever. At that moment Winnie wanted nothing more than to be in Harry's kitchen watch-

☽

21

ing his big, bossy mother cook chicken and tell them briskly to set the table and wash their hands. But she imagined Lew putting his quarter into the hospital pay phone, and dimly pictured her mother holding Daisy in the distance, small and frail, possibly dead. Winnie didn't dare leave the telephone.

"I can't. I promised I'd wait for Lew to call." Harry's voice angled away again. "She can't. She has to wait for them to call her. Yep." He turned back to Winnie: "If they call soon, tell them you're invited here. If they don't call soon, my mom will come down and bring you some supper. She says, are you worried to be there alone?"

"No." Why was it she always claimed that she was not worried—or not hungry, or not bored—when people asked her, and she sounded so responsible that they always believed her? What would happen if she had told the truth and said yes? *Yes, I'm worried and I'd like to throw up.*

"I'll be okay," said Winnie.

Winnie sat by the telephone and read comic books. She poured herself a glass of apple juice and got a box of Cheezits from the cupboard. She decided she would eat no more than four Cheezits per minute until Lew called. There were almost no Cheezits by the time the phone finally rang. Lew said the doctor had seen them; it was an ear infection, and they would be home as soon as they could; be sure the doors are locked, even though

❋

22

nothing can possibly happen. Winnie mustn't worry.

"I won't," said Winnie. "Wait a second. Harry's mom said I could come to their house for supper."

"Why don't you wait for us? We'll be back in no time."

"Okay. Bye-bye."

Winnie hung up and slowly walked to the kitchen window and looked out. An earache. That wasn't much.

She began to count the concrete squares in the driveway and rearrange them in her mind, first in groups of four, then in groups of three, the way the tiles in the bathroom floor were laid, when an odd thing happened. It suddenly seemed as if the driveway squares made a pattern, a trail that led somewhere. They had never looked that way before. Then it faded, the look of a path, and in the stillness Winnie heard a meow. She didn't want to go outside; she had promised she would keep the doors locked. But that had to be Tab's meow, and that meant Tab was out there.

She opened the window and unfastened the screen and pushed it up. She leaned way out. She had such a sure feeling that Tab was there, but she couldn't see anything the least bit catlike. Must be hiding. She ducked back inside and closed both parts of the window. What if Tab wasn't hiding? What if she had disappeared and this was her voice, calling from the nowhere or the somewhere, whatever it was, where she had gone?

☽

Winnie instantly wished she hadn't thought of that. Once last year she had been taking some medicine for a cold that wouldn't go away, and she had gotten into bed at night and heard a voice call her name. "Winnie," it had said in an everyday tone, not the least bit spooky, but right by her ear. Her mother had said it was "just the medicine," and dismissed it. But Winnie had been afraid for weeks afterward that she would hear the voice again.

She forgot to call Harry or Harry's mother. She sat as still as she possibly could, wondering if now she was hearing things. She didn't know whether to hope that she was, or hope that she wasn't. Then she heard slow, adult footsteps coming up the driveway, crunching and scraping sounds that were real. They got closer and closer, and then the back doorbell rang. Winnie jumped a mile. She ran to the door. It was Mrs. Austin.

"I've brought you a little something," she said as soon as Winnie had unlocked the door. She was a tall, heavy woman, with black hair pulled dramatically back into a perfect bun and rather glamorous clothes. Best of all, she wore eyeliner. Winnie's mother never wore any makeup except for lipstick. Mrs. Austin had an air of confident authority about her, and you didn't mind her telling you what to do; in fact, you wanted to do it.

"You'll have to put your own catsup on. I didn't know whether you like a lot or a little." Mrs. Austin handed Winnie a paper bag that held some-

☀
24

thing hot next to something cold. Winnie unrolled the top. She could see a cheeseburger—the cheese and hamburger showed through the waxed paper wrapped around it—and beside that a packet of potato chips and a plastic bag with carrot sticks and cucumber slices, and underneath those things sat a carton of chocolate milk. There was even a straw with the accordion bending place.

"It's everything I like!" Winnie cried. The queer sounds and presences in the driveway were driven from her mind. "Thanks, Mrs. Austin—really, thanks a lot!"

"Now, if it gets dark and your parents aren't back, you call me, Winifred Brown—do you promise? You can easily come stay with us in an emergency."

The very word made Winnie feel quaky all over again. She wished she could go back with Mrs. Austin right then.

"Now, will you be all right?" Harry's mother asked.

"Sure," said Winnie. "No problem."

CHAPTER
THREE
CHAPTER
THREE
CHAPTER
THREE
CHAPTER
THREE
CHAPTER
THREE
CHAPTER
THREE
CHAPTER
THREE
CHAPTER
THREE

At eight-thirty Winnie finally heard the key turn in the back door. Lew came in with Daisy cradled in his elbow. Daisy was no longer crying. Winnie's mother followed them, carrying a large, flat pizza box.

"Is she okay?" Winnie asked.

"Just a bad ear infection. She's already started on the medication," said Lew.

"She's going to be okay, isn't she?"

"Absolutely. They gave her a little medicine for the pain, too."

"I'm going to bed," said Winnie's mother. "I know I'll be up later tonight."

Lew gave Winnie's mother a kiss on the forehead. "Get some rest, dear."

"Well, Daisy!" said Winnie. "We'll take care of you. Want me to change her?"

"Sure," said Lew. "I'll put the pizza in the oven to warm up."

Winnie took Daisy from Lew, carried her into her room, unsnapped her stretch suit, and carefully extracted her arms and legs from the damp terry cloth. Then she pulled back the tapes on the Pamper, gathered it up, and tossed it into the wastebasket. It landed with a sodden thud. Lew hovered by her elbow.

"You're doing fine, just fine," he said.

"I know. I've known how to do all this stuff for ages," said Winnie. Didn't Lew realize that a twelve-year-old was practically a teenager, and teenagers were full-fledged baby-sitters?

Winnie slipped a clean undershirt over Daisy's head, and Daisy's arms suddenly floated upward. This was what her mother called the startle reflex. Winnie fastened on a fresh Pamper and picked out her favorite stretch suit, a pale green one with a little angora rabbit embroidered on the front.

"There we go!" Winnie picked her up, breathing in the sweet smell of baby lotion, or whatever it was that produced the essence of baby. Daisy was starting to cry again. Winnie handed her to Lew.

"I think she wants you."

"I think she wants something to eat," Lew said. They went out to the kitchen, and Lew put

☽

27

Daisy in her plastic baby seat on the counter, amid the dirty dishes. Her little feet twirled above three bowls of sticky cereal remains. She screamed louder. Lew searched for a clean bottle. Suddenly he shoved all the dishes to the wall with a terrible, chaotic clatter. His exasperation shocked Winnie. She was on the verge of saying that she should have cleaned everything up while she was waiting for them to come home from the doctor; but the apology wouldn't cross her lips.

"We need a maid, don't we?" she blurted.

"That's the best idea I've heard in ages," said Lew.

"Somebody like Alice on *The Brady Bunch*," said Winnie.

"Who?"

"It's a TV program."

"Mm-hmm."

Winnie knew Lew had stopped listening. Well, so what? She had some things to think about, and she needed privacy to think about them. She stood by the kitchen window looking out. Now the bottle had been found and washed and filled, and Lew had picked up Daisy. A sudden quiet fell over the kitchen. Although Lew and Daisy were right there and she could hear contented slurpings, Winnie felt enveloped by the twilight out-of-doors—the air turning a deep blue, the trees so still and deeply shadowed, and here and there a winking or a stirring in the bushes by the driveway. Things lost their everydayness: they expanded with shadows,

✺

and the dark seemed to pulse with unseen beings.

She liked to play a game with herself, imagining that the familiar things she saw had changed into other things, and then she could change them back, like the mailbox that morning. The vines overrunning the driveway curb were a waterfall, and she was looking down on it from a mountaintop; now they were vines again. She gazed out past the rear fender of the car, toward the ragged, hulking shapes of the overgrown lilacs in the next-door yard. Beyond the lilacs, the Bakers' driveway ran smoothly to the street, where an occasional jogger with a glow-in-the-dark armband ran past. Tonight something else was there, too, an animal of some kind. Winnie stiffened and blinked her eyes, straining to see what it was.

At first she made out a man in a white shirt, standing at the foot of the driveway, and then she saw a cat weaving around his ankles, the way cats will do. It looked like Tab. The cat's eyes glowed briefly in the light that fell from the neighbors' window. The man picked the cat up and stood motionless, meeting Winnie's gaze. Then he turned and was gone, and Tab with him.

"Is Mom still asleep?" Winnie asked first thing the next morning. She had come downstairs early, still in her pajamas, and found Lew and Daisy already in the kitchen. It was an overcast day, and she could smell rain. Lew must have stayed up late cleaning the kitchen. All the dishes that had been

☽

29

accumulating were washed and dried and put away. The garbage was gone, and an empty, puffy, dark green bag rustled in the trash can. The counters were clear of mail advertisements and open cereal boxes and jam-jar tops and knives with peanut butter still on them and lost sunglasses and paperback books with strange sticky places on their covers.

"Let's let her sleep as long as she can," Lew said. "I'm going in to the office late today, so I can tend to a few things for your mother." Daisy babbled in her windup swing. Lew seemed much more cheerful than he had been the night before. "What do you want for breakfast, Win? How about pancakes?"

"Oh, wow, yes!" Before her mother had had the baby, Lew used to make pancakes and bacon for the three of them on Saturday mornings. Winnie loved smelling the bacon cooking and waiting for the little pitcher of maple syrup to warm up and the pancakes to brown. Everything had become so hectic after Daisy was born that pancakes had lost out to shredded wheat, even on weekends.

Winnie went over to the swing and lifted Daisy out. Daisy's arms and legs stretched and wiggled in midair. "Hi there," said Winnie. She gave her a kiss on the head and held her against her shoulder.

Lew was pouring flour and salt and baking powder into a mixing bowl—he said pancakes made from scratch were always better—and he added some applesauce to the batter. Winnie put the baby back in her swing and wound it up.

☀

Harry called just as Lew set the first plateful of hot brown pancakes on the table. "It's me," he said when Winnie answered the phone.

"Listen, Harry, we're just starting breakfast, so can I call you back?" Steam was drifting off the top layer of pancakes, and Lew was dabbing them with butter.

"Okay. Uh, Tab didn't come back, did she?"

"Oh! I forgot about that. I think she did. And I think she belongs to someone, after all. Are you going to be home?"

"Why don't you call me when you're done."

"Okay. Bye." Winnie hung up.

Lew pulled the baby's swing next to his chair so he could keep it going without having to get up, and he and Winnie sat down at the table. The warm syrup soaked deeply into the buttered pancakes. Winnie ate a huge forkful and felt a sense of satisfaction slide down into her stomach with the pancakes.

"These are so good," she said happily.

"Now, I have a plan for this morning," said Lew. "If you'll take the baby for a walk—while it's not raining—I'm going to phone around and see about getting some household help."

"Okay! A maid! Great!"

"Not a maid; maybe a part-time housekeeper."

"I'll take Daisy up to see Harry."

"Sounds good to me."

The bacon was crisp and had a rich, smoky flavor. Winnie felt her spirits soaring practically out

☽

of sight. Sometimes everything seemed exactly right.

When they had finished breakfast, Winnie rinsed their plates and glasses, and then she called Harry. Harry's mother said she could come down and keep him company. Mrs. Austin was going to be at the clinic all day, and Jessica, one of Harry's old baby-sitters, was coming to be in charge of the household and do a few chores. Winnie ran upstairs and pulled on sneakers, a clean shirt, and a pair of shorts. A bag of favors left from a birthday party sat on the top of her bureau. She had eaten nearly all the pieces of candy, but an extra packet of M & M's caught her eye. She grabbed it, shoved it in her pocket, and ran downstairs.

Lew had pulled the big baby carriage out of the garage for her.

"Okay," said Winnie, suddenly feeling herself expand with responsibility. "I have to get the baby."

Winnie leaned over Daisy, who was cooing in her swing. This was the first time Winnie had had sole charge of her without any adult nearby. Daisy looked up, but you couldn't tell what she saw. She was so small. She couldn't do any more for herself than a toy could. She was completely helpless. Winnie must seem like a giant to Daisy—she didn't even know that Winnie was a human being! Daisy didn't know anything: only that she was hungry or full, cold or warm, cozy or not snuggled enough.

"Winnie!" called Lew. "Are you coming?"

☀

32

Winnie grabbed a cotton blanket and carried Daisy down the back steps and laid her in the carriage.

"Here I go," she said to Lew, and pushed the carriage smoothly down the driveway, right past the spot where the man had been standing.

It was only a block and a half to Harry's. She wedged the carriage against the bottom step, set the foot brake, and charged up the stairs. Daisy had fallen asleep, and Winnie could keep an eye on her from Harry's front porch.

Harry was watching television. Winnie looked through the front window screen and saw him in a television trance. She stood right in front of the window and waved both arms, as if she were signaling to an airplane pilot on a runway.

"Hey! Harry! Open the door!"

Harry looked up with a start and pushed himself to his feet. Winnie heard various keys jingling, and locks being undone, and then Harry pulled open the door and stood there, one foot bare, the other in a scruffy sock with the top drooping down to his heel.

"My mom's already left for work," Harry said, opening the screen door.

"You here by yourself?"

"Jessica's supposed to come."

"Do you have to stay here the whole time?"

"She'll kill me if I go anywhere and not tell her first."

"What about for just a few minutes?"

☽

33

"Where to?"

"Guess." Winnie put her hand over her mouth and giggled, though she wondered where the laugh had come from, because nothing was funny.

Harry looked so uncertain, so glued to the indoors, with his one bare foot and the television set chattering in the corner. A little pile of crumpled yellow cellophane bags had accumulated at the end of the couch where he had been sitting. Packs of crunchies, thought Winnie. He'd been sitting there just wolfing them down.

"Harry, sometimes you have to do things your parents don't say yes to."

"I really want to see this program."

Winnie took a look at the screen. A monster lizard was standing on its hind legs looking over the itty-bitty city.

"This does look good," Winnie said. The monster roared, and hundreds of miniature people ran to get away from it. It had well over a hundred teeth.

"I've seen this one before," said Harry.

"Is it nearly over?"

"No."

The lizard picked up a pawful of grown-ups. Their feet kicked back and forth and they screamed. The scene switched to a scientist's office.

"Want to go back to the schoolyard for just a minute?" Winnie asked. "This part looks boring."

"Pretty soon it goes back to the good stuff again."

"You said you've seen it before."

☼

The movie showed an aerial view of the narrow city streets, and a man running to escape the lizard. He was running up one street and down the next. He dashed around a corner and then doubled back up the narrow track of the street. Winnie's neck prickled. He looked like he was running through a maze.

"Harry. Come *on*. Just for a few minutes. Your mom will never know." She checked out the window to make sure Daisy's carriage was still there. "Bring that catnip thing along. Maybe we'll see Tab."

"Wait just a sec."

A dog-food commercial cut in. Harry abruptly snapped off the television set. "All right. Since you've got this compulsion."

The television pinged and crackled in the silence. Harry dug a sock out of the sofa cushions and slowly pulled it on his bare foot. He pushed both feet into his sneakers and pressed the Velcro straps shut. The calico mouse was in the middle of a tangle of magazines on the coffee table. He picked it up and put it in his pocket. He was careful to lock all the locks from the outside. Winnie eased the carriage over the curb as they crossed the street. Daisy slept on.

"Why are we doing this?" Harry asked.

"Sometimes you have to act on your instincts, Harry."

"Well, why couldn't you do it by yourself?" he grumbled.

"It's better with two."

☽

35

"Uh-oh," said Harry as they reached the corner. The sky was growing darker. Visible a block away and moving steadily toward them was a purple blob on two thin legs. "It's Jessica."

"I thought you said she was old."

As Jessica came nearer, Winnie saw that she was wearing black flats and skintight knit pants. A huge, flowered purple sweatshirt bloomed out over her bottom.

"Hi there! Where you going?" she said, hailing them cheerfully and snapping her gum. She wore big dangle earrings, purple plastic triangles that flashed brilliantly against her neck.

"Up to Earl's for cough syrup." Harry lied with surprising ease and even managed a fake cough.

"Earl's is that way," said Jessica, tilting her head.

"I know. We're going the long way around. We'll only be a few minutes. We're clean out of cough syrup, my mom says. It's good practice to go to the store on my own. I always do errands. Jessica! Really!" Jessica began to shake her head, and a grin showed the silver line of her retainer.

"Don't bother with the stories! See you guys in ten minutes, or I'm dialing 911."

Harry handed her the house keys.

"She's nice," Winnie said as they continued up the street.

"Yeah. I like Jessica. It's not like being baby-sat, you know?" They turned up Lesser Road, and

Harry dashed ahead, as if he were running a race with an invisible rival. "It's still here," he called as he went through the schoolyard's tilting gate. Harry stood a good distance away, on the opposite side of the maze. The silver lines were brighter and clearer than they had been the day before. Winnie hooked her hand over the carriage handle and pulled it to a stop, then jiggled it back and forth. The labyrinth seemed almost alive, inviting them to thread its winding curves.

"Sure is," said Winnie. The schoolyard was entirely deserted. Dark clouds stilled the air and seemed to isolate the piece of ground where they stood, the gritty asphalt with its scattering of stones and the glowing maze. Traffic noises and the metallic screech of a streetcar going around the corner sounded far away. "Well," she said, "I dare you to go into it."

"I'm not stepping into that thing," said Harry.

"I was only kidding," said Winnie. "But, hey, why not? We've got to try it out, don't you think?"

"You can."

"Well, look. Didn't we see an optical illusion? Didn't we figure that's what it was? Nothing to be scared of?"

"I'm just not that curious to find out in person, you know?"

"You were curious enough to walk over here in person, weren't you?"

"How else was I supposed to get here?"

"But, Harry!"

"You try it. You're the one that's good at mazes."

"I know. Let's send Daisy through!" Winnie gave the carriage a sharp push. Carrying Daisy, sound asleep, it rolled smoothly across the stone-strewn asphalt, crossed the silver lines and paths, and, perfectly aimed, headed straight for the center of the labyrinth.

Harry ran like mad to catch the carriage. As it crossed the lines toward the center of the maze, he pushed himself with a mighty sprint and managed just to reach the carriage handle with his fingertips. He shoved it away from the center. The carriage teetered on two wheels, then rolled on, picking up speed, until it crashed into the cyclone fence at the far end of the asphalt. It rocked on its springs, and wails burst forth like blasts from a trumpet. Winnie's heart was beating so fast, she could scarcely breathe. What had she done?

She dashed forward a couple of steps, stopped with a screech on the toes of her sneakers, changed direction, and ran around the outside of the maze. Daisy's chin vibrated with each wail, and her fists were quivering in unison with her chin. She was very red and very mad.

"Pick her up, why don't you," Harry said.

Winnie scooped out the baby and held her against her shoulder, patting her and saying, "There, there." In a moment Daisy had quieted down again. Rain started to fall in big, slow drops.

Winnie laid Daisy back in the carriage and

☀

38

pulled up the top. Gradually her fright receded, leaving her knees solid again. What on earth had come over her? She walked over to the maze and set one foot in the opening, where the outermost path began. "Do you dare me?" she said. She took a few steps. Harry hunched his shoulders, his T-shirt soaking up the rain in dark patches.

"Nothing's going to happen," Winnie said, teasing.

Harry wiped his nose on his arm. The street was empty, except for an elderly couple out walking their dachshund. The dog's tag jingled as it scurried to stay beneath its owners' umbrella.

Winnie started again, around and around, and back. This time she had no trouble following the path. A humming sound started up in her ears as she went along. She got dizzy, but not enough to make her stop. She looked back to make sure Harry was still standing there. He drifted slowly to the left in her circulating vision, looking surprised. "Winnie, come back! Don't do it!" he shouted. But now she couldn't stop. Something was pulling her. She took the last few steps to the center. The asphalt, the bent cyclone fence, the rain-soaked shrubbery all folded together. She had a sensation of being squeezed too tightly, and then the school-yard shattered into bright shards that fell away to nothing.

☽

CHAPTER FOUR

CHAPTER FOUR
CHAPTER FOUR
CHAPTER FOUR
CHAPTER FOUR
CHAPTER FOUR
CHAPTER FOUR
CHAPTER FOUR

Winnie stood in a ragged clearing surrounded by overgrown, sharp-needled hedges so dark a green, they were almost black. They were tall, reaching far above her, twice as high as her head, and their thick, reddish roots dug into the ground like gnarled hands. She couldn't see anything beyond them. They were as thick as a wood. Above her, there was a perfectly blue sky, a summer-picnic sky. She felt a moment of panic. This was like being in prison.

She was standing beside a sundial. Across the clearing a faded wooden structure tilted sideways, an old gazebo with weeds sprouting through its benches. Next to it was a small pond covered with green scum, a stand of cattails crowding up one end. A stone bench sat crookedly by, almost consumed by weeds.

There was not a sign of a human being anywhere. A mosquito whined around her ear, then lit on the back of her knee and bit viciously. She swatted at it, but a pale welt sprang up, anyway. She always reacted to insect bites—"Bites really take on you," the school nurse had once said to her at a picnic. She would be in for some awful itching, and she had nothing to put on it.

Harry should be coming through any moment now. It seemed as if she had already been here for hours, but when she looked at her watch, she saw that it couldn't have been more than a minute or two—it was still eight-forty.

"Harry?" she called out.

She could have sworn she heard a ripple of whispers run around the clearing. "Who's there?" she cried, turning around. She scanned the dark circle of evergreens, but there was no further sound. She thought she saw something move in the distance—something blue, like Harry's shirt, against the wall of black and green. She ran toward the color. Against the hedges there was a shimmering place in the air, but when she got closer, the shimmering stopped. There was nobody there.

"I'm so dumb! I should've grabbed him!" she said out loud. Unless, of course, there was nothing to grab. Her voice sounded high and screechy with suppressed tears. In the silence that followed, she thought she heard an echo, a voice mocking hers.

☽

But maybe not. Her ears were full of her own pulse. Sweat was forming on her neck and scalp. The circle of sky overhead was still intensely blue, and the air was getting hotter. The smell of cedar was stifling.

Winnie began to feel sick to her stomach. She lay down flat on her back. Under her shoulder blades the lumpy knots of crabgrass felt comfortingly familiar. Her stomach immediately improved. She felt a little shaky, and she was suddenly terribly thirsty, but the shaky feeling did not get worse.

Where was she? It was easier to think lying down. She held her wrist up and looked at her watch. It still said eight-forty. Now she noticed that the second hand was no longer moving. She shook her arm, but the hand still didn't move.

This didn't look like the place that had the Egyptian crocodiles, she was pretty sure of that. On the other hand, it just might be the Land of the Dead. She had seen plenty of hedges like these in cemeteries, and little stone benches and pools, too. What if there were ghosts and shades all around her, invisible, watching her, waiting for her to catch on to what had happened, waiting for her to make some mistake so that she would have to stay with them forever?

She didn't want them to be invisible. She didn't care if they were white or transparent, but she did want to be able to see them.

If she kept lying down, flat on her back, they might mistake her for one of them. She sat up. She was feeling better now. She got on her feet and looked around cautiously. If there were gravestones, she wanted to know just where they were so she wouldn't accidentally step on them and insult their occupants.

She tiptoed across the clearing through patches of white-headed dandelions and stepped into the gazebo. The floorboards were half broken, and feather-topped weeds stuck up through them and tickled her legs. A papery gray wasp's nest was fastened to the underside of the roof. A bench ran around the interior of the little house, and a bundle of cloth lay in a heap under one section of it. Winnie bent over to look at the cloth, but she didn't want to pick it up. It had faded, and she could see that it had been a small quilt or baby's coverlet. She was afraid that if she shook it, something alive would run out.

She stepped back out of the gazebo. Being scared was making her thirstier by the minute. She walked over to the pond and looked in. It could be poisonous. It was choked with green weeds and lily pads, and moss hung in filmy, green clouds below its surface. The water was full of murky life; it was hard to see what was there.

She wasn't that thirsty yet. Once Harry got here, they could decide together about drinking the water.

Once Harry got here . . . Panic, banging around in her mind like a bird in a closed room, was only a thought away. What if Harry didn't come through at all? What if she was stuck here?

☽

She didn't see any signs of the maze anywhere. What if it was a one-way maze? She pictured the story in *Newsweek*: GIRL VANISHES IN LOCAL SCHOOLYARD. MAZE BLAMED. There would be a photograph of her mother and Lew, looking anxiously into the camera, and an interview with Harry. Harry, as the last person to have seen her alive, would get lots of attention. A prickle of jealousy rose along the back of her neck. She wondered if Harry had gone back to his house by now, and whether he had pushed Daisy home.

She was so thirsty that the insides of her cheeks were sticking to her gums, and her tongue made a crackling sound when she tried to lick her lips. There was a spot on one bank of the pond that had no green stuff growing on it. She knelt down and looked into it. A frog plopped into the water nearby, making a juicy splash. If it was good for the frog, why wouldn't it be good for her? She dipped her hands in, brought up a palmful of water, and slurped it down. It had a greenish taste, but she took several more gulps, anyhow. It couldn't be as bad as those toxic wells she was always hearing about on television.

A swampy aftertaste filled her mouth. There was no point in even thinking about a toothbrush. Then she remembered the M & M's. They would surely take the awful taste away. She reached into her pocket, drew out the packet, and tore open one end. The crisp, candy-coated circles with their dense, chocolate interiors canceled out the odd taste. She ate the entire package just to be sure.

She brushed the twigs off her shorts, cast a glance around the clearing, and saw a place where she might be able to pick out a path. She pressed her way in, ducking and bending, shoving the larger branches out of her face. Far away, she heard human voices. She tried to peer ahead through the thick greenery, but all she could see were tangles of roots and a blur of needles. The sound of her footsteps was muffled by a thick layer of fallen needles. In the quiet she heard the voices getting closer.

A sickish feeling crept into her stomach. She pushed away the memory of the M & M's. She looked up, and the part of the sky that she could see seemed to make a quarter turn to the left. Her arms and legs were itching. She pushed on, but she didn't seem to be getting anywhere. She looked up into some towering evergreens, massed together before and behind her. She couldn't tell which direction was in and which was out. Off to the right a tall figure, entirely white, loomed out of the arched branches. She pushed frantically through the underbrush, away from the figure, slapping at twigs and brambles and thorny branches, forcing her bare legs through bushes whose sharp twigs dug into her skin.

"I've got to get out of here!" she shouted. This place was horrible, and she'd probably end up getting eaten by monsters. The thought of eating made a fresh wave of nausea rise in her stomach. She crouched down on her hands and knees. The hedges seemed to be falling, falling, falling toward

☽

her, but never quite falling over. She pushed herself to her feet again and saw a broken fence, and daylight beyond it. She stumbled across the last few yards and grabbed the crosspiece of the fence. It was only half as tall as she was—the rest had rotted away—but she wasn't sure she could make it over, her legs were so shaky. If she could get half of herself over . . . one leg, one arm, her stomach . . . and she rolled and fell to the grass on the other side. She stood up, took a few steps, and the entire space where she was standing floated once around her, tilted up, and smacked her in the face.

She must have fainted, for the next thing she knew, she was lying facedown on the ground with grass caught in her teeth. Her nose hurt, and tears squeezed themselves out from beneath her eyelids. Stupid Harry! Why hadn't he managed to make it through? All of this was his fault. If he were here now, he'd be able to go for help. She closed her eyes and tears flooded down. "Rats!" she said.

Someone tapped her on the back.

Winnie raised her head, which felt as if it weighed a thousand pounds, and looked over her shoulder into the kindly face of a girl about her own age. Behind her knelt a severe-looking woman wearing a black dress with a small white collar. She was frowning and shaking her head, and Winnie thought she heard her say, "So it's finally happened."

☀

CHAPTER FIVE

Winnie lay on her back on a hard, narrow bed in a small room. The walls were covered with flowered paper, little cornflower-blue nosegays marching in diagonals up to the ceiling, and a quilt was pulled up to her chin. Her stomach felt terrible, but fortunately it was at quite a distance from her brain, and if she just lay still, it might not notice that she was awake. A clean cinnamon smell came from the sheets.

"Are you awake?" A face appeared over hers, inches away. It was the same girl Winnie had seen earlier. She had pale skin and blond braids and an old-fashioned white blouse trimmed with ruffles.

Winnie nodded.

"Are you feeling better?"

Winnie nodded again, not sure what her voice would sound like. She couldn't remember how she'd gotten to this bed.

"You've been here for two days."

Winnie lurched upright. "How long?" she croaked. The room gave a quick spin around her, and she clutched at the edges of the mattress. She was wearing something with long sleeves.

"Two days. Don't you remember any of it?"

"No," Winnie whispered, straining her memory to bring back anything at all.

"You've been very ill. Aunt Harriet nursed you herself. I could hear you talking, but Aunt Harriet wouldn't let me listen. She said I couldn't come in until you were awake."

"I was talking?"

"You were delirious, Aunt Harriet calls it. That's when you go out of your mind, and you have a high fever, and you think you're somewhere else or the people around you are someone else."

Maybe she was still delirious. "I can't remember any of that."

She liked this girl, but she wanted her to turn into Harry, and the room into her own room. Winnie squeezed her eyes shut, hoping she would see something different when she opened them.

Another whiff of cinnamon floated past her nose. She looked again. The room was the same. It was small, and the furniture in it looked ordinary and a little worn. The border of the sheet beneath her fingers was neatly mended with a tiny, square patch. The quilt smoothed across her body was faded, one edge frayed and feathery with loose threads. Quiet bars of sunlight fell across the floor. White, gauzy curtains were pulled partway across the window.

"We found you outside the maze," the girl said. "Do you remember that? You were flat on the ground. Swamp fever, Aunt Harriet says. Probably bit by a swamp mosquito. Others have had it. Do you still feel hot?"

The girl pressed her hand to Winnie's forehead. "No. Fever's gone. But you can't get up yet. Aunt Harriet says one full day in bed after the fever's gone, and plenty of broth and bread to build up your strength."

Winnie nodded. "Is Harry here?"

"Harry?"

"We came together. . . ." Then she remembered. They hadn't come together.

"Where did you come from? We didn't see anyone else. How did you get into the maze?"

"What maze?"

"That's where we found you. It's not really a maze anymore, but it used to be one a long time ago, a garden maze with benches and statues. All the hedges and bushes are grown into tangles, and it's full of weeds and a horrid, smelly pond. Aunt Harriet says she doesn't want me even to go in it. How did you get there?"

"I was lost," said Winnie.

"Where from? Who are you?"

"I'm trying to figure it out. I must have hit my head." She was starting to remember the last two days: a hazy recollection of someone helping her sit up; of a chamber pot, that's what it must have been, a large china dish she had to sit on—how embarrassing, though it hadn't seemed so at the time; of someone putting cool cloths on her face and giving her sips of water.

"What's your name? You must remember that!"

"Winnie Brown."

"I'm Lily Taylor. I don't live here, I'm just staying with my Aunt Harriet for the summer. She's my father's younger sister. Our house is in Greening. That's fifty miles away. Have you ever been there?"

Winnie shook her head.

"It's only a village. That's where we live, but my father goes to the city with his business affairs. He and my mother went to Europe for the summer. Crescent Ridge is my father's real home, that's what he says."

"Crescent Ridge?"

"Right here! This is Crescent Ridge. Where Aunt Harriet lives. It used to be my grandparents' house. They were rich, but we're not. They're the ones who had the maze. They died before I was born. They were lost at sea. They were returning from a trip to Europe, and their ship broke up in a storm and everyone drowned. And they lost all their trunks as well, with all the beautiful things they were bringing back."

"That's terrible. I wouldn't like to drown."

"They say it's not a bad death," said Lily thoughtfully. "I often try to decide which would be the best way to die. I guess in your sleep. That's what I'd choose."

"Yes, but with a little bit of warning."

Winnie looked at Lily's clothes, and Lily looked back at Winnie, and then they both laughed with embarrassment.

"These aren't my clothes," said Winnie, holding out her arms.

Lily shook her head. "Clara's washing your underthings."

"My underthings?" Did she mean Winnie's shorts and T-shirt?

"We didn't see any of your other clothes. Did—did someone rob you?"

"I don't know."

"Well, don't think about it if they did."

"My watch! Where is it?" Her wrists were bare.

"Is this it?" Lily slid off the bed, opened the top bureau drawer, and handed Winnie her wrist-watch. Winnie saw that Lily's skirt came far below her knees, and a feeling of dread clogged her throat.

"Papa has a beautiful pocket watch, but I've never seen one like this. Are you very rich?"

☽

"I'm not at all rich," said Winnie. She fastened the watch. It was still stuck at eight-forty. "All kinds of people have these where I come from. Is the maze far from here, by the way?"

"You can see it from this window."

"Lily!" called a voice from somewhere else in the house.

Lily jumped up. "I'll be back. Do you want something to eat? Aunt Harriet told me to come see if you were awake. We'll get you back home, don't worry. I shouldn't say it, but I'm glad you're lost here. I do love Aunt Harriet, but I haven't anyone to talk to."

When she was sure Lily was gone, Winnie sat up gingerly and swung her legs to the side of the bed. Her queasy feeling swam back full force. If she hadn't sat up for two days, no wonder she felt funny. Something in the pond must have poisoned her. A green shiver ran through her at the memory of the brackish water. Her head felt as light and empty as a cartoon balloon.

There was a large china pitcher in an enormous bowl on a wooden stand a few feet away from the bed. There was water in it, but when she tried to lift it, it was too heavy to budge. She didn't see a glass or a paper cup, anyway. A damp cloth hung from a rail on the side of the stand.

She got back into bed. She felt awful, probably because she was so hungry. If only they'd left her some crackers or ginger ale, the way her mother did when she got the stomach flu.

She pulled the covers back up to her chin and looked up at the ceiling. There was no overhead light, and no bedside lamp, either—just a half-burned candle in a holder on the bureau.

She was trying to think of a way to get some food when the woman she had seen before, the one in black, stepped silently into the room and came toward her. She was thin and ramrod-straight. Her hair was pulled up into a severe bun at the top of her small head, a head that looked even smaller because it sat on top of a long, thin neck. If this was Aunt Harriet, no wonder Lily wanted someone to talk to.

"You may want some soup and a slice or two of bread," the woman said in a dry voice. "Here they are." She set the tray down on the table beside Winnie's bed. The delicious smell of soup and fresh bread reached Winnie's nose. She sat up and reached for the tray. She saw that the woman's skirt nearly reached the floor.

"Thank you," she said. The woman stood next to her bed, watching. Winnie took a bite of the bread. "Thank you for bringing me this," she said uneasily. "It's delicious."

"Clara makes the bread." She kept staring at Winnie. "You're lucky we found you before the fever was too far gone. How did you come to be out there?"

"I can't remember," said Winnie. Each time she repeated it, it sounded less convincing to her own ears.

☽

"You've got amnesia, then."

"I can remember my name, and that's it. I'm not sure how I got here or who my family is. The fever, it must be."

"Yes. The fever. We'll find out sooner or later. You're not to leave this room until you are entirely better. You'll do as you're told, won't you?"

The woman gave Winnie a crisp stamp of a look and left the room. When Winnie could no longer hear her footsteps, she carefully placed the tray on the table and slid off the bed. She had hardly ever tasted homemade bread. It and the soup had already begun to take effect. She felt as if her bones had soaked them right up and that she was strong enough to stand and walk around. She wolfed down the remaining piece of bread and then tiptoed around to the window and pulled back the curtain. A long swath of grass dropped down past a barn and some sheds and ran to the edge of a densely wooded thicket, blackish green and shapeless. That was it. There was no maze.

Winnie crawled back under the covers, shivering. There was a woods but no maze. Where was she? She must be in a farmhouse. The cotton quilt and the rag rug and the simple furniture reminded her of her grandparents' house in the country. But they'd have given her Campbell's chicken-noodle soup and a peanut-butter sandwich. And the clothes that Lily and this Aunt Harriet wore were strange. They were like the clothes in photographs of people in another century.

Winnie felt cold prickles scuttle like crabs across her shoulder blades. Of course she couldn't be in another century. Maybe these people were members of a religious sect and had to wear special clothing. Furthermore, she was hungry again, and that was a good sign. That's what her mother always said when Winnie was sick.

The door opened. "Here's Aunt Harriet," said Lily. "I told her you had finally woken up."

A short, slender woman stepped into the room behind Lily. She had curly blond hair, hair so unruly that it stuck out all around her face in corkscrews, and lively green eyes, and she looked young, nowhere near Winnie's mother's age, which was forty. So this was Aunt Harriet! She bent over the bed and looked into Winnie's face. She, too, was wearing an old-fashioned dress, of silky, gray-blue material, with long, tight sleeves and lace around the neck. "There, now," she said. "Feeling more like yourself, I should think. I am Lily's Aunt Harriet." She sat down on the edge of the bed. "Who are you?"

"Winnie Brown."

"I'm sure your parents must be anxious about you, Winnie Brown. Where do you live? We must send a message and arrange for your return."

Winnie couldn't think of a thing to say. Her mouth dropped open stupidly; she couldn't get any words out.

"What's the matter? You don't need to be frightened of us." Aunt Harriet seemed so nice,

Winnie wanted to tell her. But what if she thought Winnie was a lunatic? Winnie's eyes filled with tears, and Aunt Harriet patted her hand.

"Are you afraid they will be angry?" Aunt Harriet asked.

Winnie shook her head.

"But something prevents you from going home?"

Winnie nodded.

"I'd like to help you if I can. Perhaps there are things you find it difficult to say. Have you run away from home, for instance? Your home can't be that far from Crescent Ridge or you'd have arrived in much worse condition than you did. You can talk to me later. We mustn't let your family go on worrying, though. And you mustn't do any more running away. I am responsible for you now."

Aunt Harriet stood up and looked at Winnie's tray. Her clothes were immaculately ironed, her small hands neat and soft. "I shall ask Violet to bring you more soup. By tomorrow you should be up and about. We will talk again this evening." She smiled—a good smile but with something very firm in it.

"I'll bring her the soup," said Lily.

"Good. You've been wanting company, and I've been distracted these past few days." As she left the room she gave Winnie an appraising look, which Winnie did her best not to shrink back from.

Winnie consumed the second bowl of soup while Lily watched her.

※

"I've got to get up," she said when the last drop was gone. "I'm sure I can stand up without feeling dizzy."

Winnie swung her legs over the side of the bed and stood up. So far, so good. She walked over to the window and pulled the curtain to one side. She wanted to keep that patch of woods within seeing range. She had to ask a question.

"What time is it?" she asked.

"Afternoon."

"What day is it?"

"Thursday."

"But which Thursday?"

"The one that comes after Wednesday!"

"No, no, what's the date?"

"It's June 19, 1889."

Winnie reached for the windowsill. Her legs began to wobble as if they belonged to somebody else.

"Ooh, you're so shaky!" said Lily.

Winnie looked down at her knees, which were literally knocking together. She had never seen them do this before. She dived back into the bed and pulled up the quilt. "Your aunt seems so nice. I hope she can help me." Now her teeth were chattering.

"She will. You mean, your mind is still a blank?"

"Yes," Winnie whispered.

"What if you've done something terrible and your mind has blotted it out! Maybe you're in

57

hiding. You don't look like a murderer."

"What do I look like?"

"Well, rather odd, though it's hard to say exactly what it is. Your hair is so short, for one thing. Did it get cut off because you were sick? Or were you in disguise as a boy?"

"No, this is the way I usually look."

Winnie's legs were slowing down now. She sat up. "I've got a good idea. Why don't we go out and look in the maze? Maybe that will make me remember."

"Well, Aunt Harriet won't let you get up yet, and I know she won't let you in the maze."

"But I'm getting better. I get over things fast. I only had the flu for half a day when it was going around at school."

"The flu? People die of influenza," said Lily. There was a shocked silence. Then Lily got to her feet. "I promised I wouldn't stay long. You're supposed to rest some more." She looked at Winnie for a long time and then asked, "Do you believe in ghosts?"

"Not really, n-no."

"I do. I've seen 'em lots of times." And she left the room.

In a few moments, though she was sure she was perfectly well, Winnie fell asleep again. In her dreams things rustled and creaked, and a dark shape stood by her bed, nudging the mattress. Whispers flew around her ears, then vanished with a sigh. When she awoke, it was raining.

CHAPTER SIX

CHAPTER SIX

CHAPTER SIX

CHAPTER SIX

CHAPTER SIX

CHAPTER SIX

CHAPTER SIX

CHAPTER SIX

Winnie sat straight up. She felt much better now. She got out of bed and pulled the window curtain to one side. A dash of rain turned the glass to ripples of water, and she couldn't see anything clearly.

She sat on the bed again, trying to think. She hated feeling trapped in one room. She decided she would just look down the hall, to see what was there. She stood inside the threshold, so she was literally staying in her room, and hung on to the door frame and leaned out. She saw a long, narrow corridor with several doors, all of them closed. Well, it wouldn't hurt to walk quickly down to the end and back. She could always say she heard a noise that scared her. With every step the floor-boards creaked, but there seemed to be no one to hear. At the end of the corridor a steep, narrow staircase led down, turning out of sight. She could hear kitchen noises at the bottom—dishes clinking, the splash of water, a chair scraping. Then people talking: "It's just a village tale," said a man in a thick, wheezy voice.

"It's not just a tale," said a woman. It sounded like the woman in the black dress.

"Magic powers and ancient curses. Maybe it's an ancient blessing! Maybe it's a lot of malarkey. Your Great-aunt Sally is a meddler, that's all she is. Is there another biscuit, by the way?"

"She has insights, Alfred."

"Yes, dear."

"You wouldn't know an insight if it was left on your breakfast plate!"

"If there was one on my breakfast plate, I'd know what to do with it."

Through the swash of heavy rain came a crack of lightning, a white blast that silenced the two voices at the foot of the stairs.

"That was a near one," the man said.

Two bright flashes filled the dark corridor where Winnie stood—white light seemed to press against the narrow window at the end of the hall. Winnie shut her eyes and ducked. There was a crack, and the floor shook. Winnie heard a scolding voice: "Alfred, you're still afraid of a little thunder and lightning!"

Winnie sympathized with Alfred. She ran back to her room. What did they do about lightning in the old days? Was there a lightning rod? She stood by the window. Lightning flashed again, this time illuminating the woods. For a split second, before the dark and rain closed in, Winnie thought she saw the curves of a maze within the woods.

The door to her room suddenly opened, and a girl backed in holding a tray. She might have been sixteen or seventeen, and she had dark hair gathered into a bun and red cheeks. She looked rattled, as if carrying a tray made her nervous. "Here's your supper," she said. Another bowl of soup and two pieces of toast lay skimpily on a plate.

Winnie stared in dismay at the tray. "I'm awfully hungry."

"She's going to eat with me!" said Lily, skipping through the doorway. "Aunt Harriet says she's well enough."

"All right." The girl sighed.

"Mrs. Minot says bring the tray back down."

"All right," the girl said again and took the tray away.

"Who is that?" Winnie asked Lily.

"That's Clara. She helps Mrs. Minot, and Mrs. Minot is the housekeeper. Mrs. Minot's been here for ages; she even worked for my grandparents when she was a little girl. She's devoted to my aunt. She runs everything. She's married to Alfred, and he's supposed to be in charge of the grounds, only his arthritis always bothers him. He's nice

☽

when she isn't around. They don't have any children. Mrs. Minot takes care of me when Aunt Harriet is away."

"Does she go away often?"

"Lately, yes. Aunt Harriet had this awful thing happen . . ." Lily paused and looked expectantly at Winnie.

"What awful thing?"

"Ssh!"

A tuneless humming came up the staircase, and Clara appeared. "Your Aunt Harriet says to tell you she is waiting."

The delicious smell of roast meat filled the corridor. Winnie thought she would keel right over if she didn't get some real food, and fast.

"You can't come down in a nightgown," said Lily.

"Where are my clothes?"

"You weren't wearing very many."

"Well, what about the ones I was wearing?"

"They're probably still drying. Let me see what I can give you. You're a lot taller than I am."

Winnie found her sneakers in the bottom of the wardrobe that stood in one corner. "What awful thing?" she repeated as she pulled them on. Never mind socks.

"I'll tell you later. I've never seen any shoes like those." They were big red basketball sneakers that made Winnie's feet look yards long.

"They're good for running," said Winnie.

Lily took Winnie down the hallway and into

the room where she slept. There was a big brass bed covered with a white quilt, a bureau, and a small mirror. In one corner stood a trunk with a rounded top made of shiny metal with designs stamped in it. Lily pulled a green-checked dress from the closet. Winnie held it up against herself. "Well, I'll try it," she said.

The sleeves were so narrow, Winnie could only bend her elbows partway, and Lily had to leave the top several hooks unfastened, but finally it was more on than off.

"Let's go. At least you're dressed," said Lily. She led Winnie down the front stairs, a carved oak staircase that turned past an enormous arched window. Winnie looked out across rolling lawns and glimpsed a lake in the dreary blue twilight. She had the fleeting impression that she had seen it before.

The dining room was huge. Winnie sat across from Lily at a great dark table the size of a ship's deck. Aunt Harriet sat at the head. Winnie unfolded a heavy white linen napkin and laid it across her lap. A lace tablecloth covered the acres between her plate and Lily's; she could see mended places in the cloth, and the edges of her napkin hem were frayed. Cobwebs hung in the ceiling corners; the light wasn't very good—six feeble candles fluttered in a candelabra in the center of the table, and the wood paneling on the walls seemed to swallow up the remaining light.

The door to the kitchen swung open, and

☽

Clara brought in a tray of soup bowls. It was celery soup, explained Aunt Harriet. Winnie tasted a spoonful. It didn't have much flavor.

"You're looking much better, Winnie," said Aunt Harriet.

"I'm almost back to my old self," said Winnie.

"That's good. And how about your amnesia? Your memory will come back, I'm sure of it. You don't think you ran away from home, do you?"

"I couldn't have. I'm not that type."

"What type are you?"

"I'm the timid type, actually." It was true, when she thought about it. "And I'm the stay-at-home type." She remembered how it had felt when Lew put his arm around her and asked her to be a good sport. Nobody here was going to stretch and yawn with a terrible noise to see if they could make her laugh. She suddenly wasn't hungry anymore.

"So you remember that much. Can you recall what your home is like? Who is there?"

"Well, I can remember my mother's face, and my stepfather, and we have a baby named Daisy. I can see us all in the kitchen, around the table."

"And is the fire burning? Is this a cottage where you live?"

She would have to be careful. "I can't seem to picture this part. All I can remember is when I came through the maze." She was taking a chance, but she had to see what would happen if she told the truth.

☀

64

Clara moved around the table collecting their soup bowls. She took them to the kitchen and returned with a platter holding the roast lamb. It was a rich, dark brown, piping hot, and surrounded by golden roast potatoes. Aunt Harriet began to carve the meat.

"You came through our old maze?" Aunt Harriet said. "How could you? The maze has been fenced in for years. It's nothing but a tangle of woods now. There's a bog in the center, and the whole place is infested with insects and snakes and poison ivy. William warned us to keep people out of it. He was in charge of the grounds here." Her voice cracked, and she stopped talking; her own words had brought her to a halt. "Now, what was I saying about the maze? Well, you must have come upon it from the other side through the open fields there, up from the road. And then you climbed over the fence. Difficult but not impossible."

She hadn't understood. Winnie took a deep breath. "That's not what I meant. I came through the maze, from where I live, which happens to be—I'm not sure you want to hear this, but anyway, it happens to be in the next century, I'm sorry to say." She heard herself apologize, as if that would soften the shock. "I guess I do have my memory back now."

"I think it's your fever you've got back, not your memory," said Aunt Harriet.

"No, I feel fine!"

☽

"Then you must have had a vivid hallucination. I can tell that you believe you are telling the truth. When you've had a good night's sleep, you'll be able to sort it out."

Lily was looking at Winnie, excitement burning two red circles on her cheeks. "You came backward a hundred years?"

"Yes. And now I guess I'm stuck here."

"A hundred years? But that's what— You really did? What did it feel like?"

"That's enough, Lily," said Aunt Harriet.

"But, Aunt Harriet! Mrs. Minot is always saying the maze has secret powers. You know the stories village people tell."

"Lily, that's nonsense. I've heard the village tales, but I don't put much stock in them. Perhaps Mrs. Minot believes she knows something special about the maze—she's been here so long, she's entitled to think what she wishes. The maze *is* dangerous. Once we had a tragedy there, Winnie. Two little boys were presumed to have drowned in the pool. After that the maze was closed off."

"Tell her the rest!" said Lily. "Tell her about the maze they found."

Aunt Harriet smiled and shook her head at Lily. "Oh, very well. Before I was born, my parents had this garden maze laid out and planted at the bottom of the lawn for the amusement of the village children. It was a great piece of work— dozens of gardeners, and men laying paths of rose-colored gravel, and marble brought from Europe for statues, and they even dug a pond in the center.

"It took two years to complete. When the workmen first began to lay out the maze design, they found a maze already there. Some trenches had been dug a long time ago in the ground, and they formed a big, curving maze, by then mostly overgrown with grass. No one had ever noticed it, though it seemed to have been there for many years. So they laid out the garden maze along the lines of the trenches. They were filled in, of course, so that no one could stumble over them.

"When it was finally done, Mother and Father invited children to come on Sunday afternoons and go through the maze, and the children's parents came, too, with picnic lunches. This went on for some years, and then the accident happened, and after that my parents wouldn't let anyone near the maze. I was only a baby then, but my older brother, Charles, Lily's father, remembers it clearly. Violet was actually in the maze that day, and she apparently saw them drown. I think it made a terrible impression on her, as of course it would on anyone. She was only nine.

"Now, I expressly forbid either of you to go into the maze, and I shall tell Mrs. Minot so particularly before I leave. I shall be going out of town, as Lily knows, for a few days. Shall we have dessert?" She rang a little bell beside her dinner plate. After a disastrous-sounding crash in the kitchen Clara burst into the dining room. "Please,

☽

Miss Taylor, now there is only one piece of cottage cake for dessert, and who is to get it?"

Aunt Harriet laughed. "Divide it between the two girls. I shall have just coffee in the library, please."

The cake was bland and not very sweet. Winnie wished she had saved a few of her M & M's.

Aunt Harriet had the children come sit with her in the library. She poured herself a small glass of dark gold liquid with a sharp odor. "I must say it, Winnie," she began, sitting down in a deep wing chair. "The clothes you came in are very strange, hardly appropriate. I never have seen any like them. I can't imagine where such skimpy clothes could be acceptable. And the label—'Made in Taiwan.' Where is Taiwan? It doesn't sound like Massachusetts."

"I don't know exactly where it is," said Winnie truthfully. "But we all wear clothes like this in 1989."

"You are persistent, aren't you? Tomorrow I shall lend you some clothes. That dress would have fit you about two years ago! You're a good deal taller than Lily. Perhaps I have something that will suit. Now, if your memory doesn't come back, what are we to do with you?"

"It *has* come back."

"She can stay here until it does, can't she?" asked Lily.

"Yes, of course. I would hate to turn you over to an orphanage."

☀

Winnie shivered at the thought. She had read about orphanages in novels, and she could picture the long wooden tables with dull bowls of porridge, children clothed in colorless smocks going to morning prayers, having to sew all day.

"Now you're shivering," said Aunt Harriet. "I'm sure your fever is back, and I've kept you up too late. You must both go to bed."

"Not now!" said Lily. "There must be a doctor who knows about amnesia. I shall make inquiries when I go to the city. I am making my trip the day after tomorrow. I had thought to postpone it, but it is wiser not to. I need to visit my lawyers about some complicated matters, business you would find very dull if I described it. If I hear any reports of a child missing from a good family, then we will have some hope of sending you home. Or perhaps your memory will return spontaneously."

"I feel a whole lot better than I did, that's for sure!" It was better not to argue—she didn't want to antagonize Aunt Harriet.

"Are you going to look for William in the city?" asked Lily.

"I am going to hire a private investigator to help us find William." Aunt Harriet took a sip of the gold liquor. She cleared her throat and was silent for a few minutes.

"What happened to him?" asked Winnie in a whisper.

"We don't know. He was last seen around

☽

noontime some three weeks ago, and he never came in after that. Young Thomas—that's his helper—was the last one to see him. I assumed he had gone to the village on an errand. I still think he might have, and met with an accident, but someone would have found him by now. Perhaps he has sustained a blow on the head and has amnesia, like you. All his things are still here, everything just as he left it in his rooms. The only things missing are his boots and the clothes he worked in. That's all we know."

"We've looked for him everywhere," Lily added.

"Everywhere," said Aunt Harriet. "Now to bed, both of you."

She kissed Lily on the forehead and pressed Winnie's hand. As they left the library Winnie saw her turn back and stare into the fire, a look of sadness and longing on her face.

Winnie lay in bed for a long time without falling asleep. Her narrow bed and the square, brown bureau and stiff little chair and half-burned candle all pressed a foreignness upon her that she could hardly bear. Tomorrow she would ask Lily more about the village tales, whatever they were, and she would ask Mrs. Minot about the maze that used to be there. Her throat went dry at the thought of asking Mrs. Minot anything.

Winnie got out of bed and stepped to the window. Mrs. Minot had told her to keep it closed, because in this household they didn't believe the "night airs" were healthy. Winnie shoved it up and propped it open with her shoe. If Harry had only come through, they could talk to Mrs. Minot together. But Harry hadn't. At least tomorrow she would have her own clothes back. If she were wearing her right clothes, surely it would be easier to find her way home.

The window was still fogged over from being closed against the rain. Winnie drew a maze on it with her finger—around and around, in and out, toward the center. She wondered how close the drawing was to the maze outside, and she wished now she had thought to memorize the schoolyard path.

CHAPTER
SEVEN

CHAPTER
SEVEN

CHAPTER
SEVEN

CHAPTER
SEVEN

CHAPTER
SEVEN

CHAPTER
SEVEN

CHAPTER
SEVEN

CHAPTER
SEVEN

It felt like hours before Winnie fell asleep, yet she woke up just as the sky was getting light. She tiptoed to the window. White mist lay in shreds across the lawn and hid the bottom of the slope, where the woods rose through it like a castle in the distance. Overhead, the sky was a smooth, pearly pink.

Winnie couldn't hear any noise in the house. Picking up her sneakers, she crept down the kitchen stairs in her bare feet. She pushed through the back door, closed it behind her, and sat down in a chilly huddle on the stone stoop. She pulled on her sneakers. If she could just get one good look at the maze in daylight, maybe she could find some trace of a path.

She started across the grass. It was soaking wet, and her nightgown was soon flapping clammily around her ankles. When she reached the gate, she glanced back over her shoulder and realized she was looking at what was going to be the Dunfey Nursing Home in a hundred years. Crescent Ridge was the estate Mrs. Austin had told them about. And that meant that her own house was only two blocks away: two blocks and a century. She stared into the distance at some green fields, nightmarishly empty of what she most wanted to see: Mrs. Karabedian's driveway, the tarry cracks in the street where her bicycle bumped, her own gray house with the rickety back door.

Winnie scrambled over the broken gate. In the shrubbery before her there was no path, no order. It seemed a malignant overgrowth, swarming with branches and sharp needles. The first barrier of thickets near the fence led to dense evergreens, grown together in shapeless tangles. As she pushed through she had to blink and squint to keep branches from poking her in the eye. The ground was uneven, ridged with gullies that made it hard to walk. She nearly screamed when she came upon a woman, all in white, standing on the other side of a tangle of branches. The woman was made of stone. A statue. The statue stared at nothing with blank, benign eyes. A stone bench faced Winnie, and beyond that she could see a pair

☽

of statues, a boy and a girl. They were wearing wreaths and holding hands. Stains and moss ran down one side of the boy's head, and their joined hands were twined above with dark-leaved vines.

It was too quiet in the maze. There was nothing to go by underfoot—no silver paint, no pink stone paths. Panic began to race through Winnie's brain: *I'll never get back, it's gone for good, I'll never get back, it's gone for good.*

The sun had risen by now, and its reddish light fell in pencil-straight lines through the mist. Birds chirped and called overhead: a perfectly normal day. Winnie turned back toward the gate. Aunt Harriet might be up already, and if she found out that Winnie had gone into the maze, there was no telling what she might do.

Winnie picked her way back to the gate and hurried up the slope toward the house. There she saw the thin figure of Mrs. Minot, bent over like a hairpin, working at the edge of the kitchen garden. Mrs. Minot straightened up amid the rows of tiny green sprouts and looked over at Winnie as if not at all surprised to see her.

"Up early, I see," she said.

"Yes." Winnie's teeth began to chatter.

"And soaking wet."

Winnie nodded.

"Come into the kitchen. Clara's just stirring up the fire. You'll catch your death like that." Mrs. Minot put down her trowel and gloves. "I often get

※

74

up this early," she said. "I get up with the first light of dawn. Things look so different at this time of day, don't you think?"

"Mmm," said Winnie, trying to sound calm. She had told herself that she had to talk to Mrs. Minot; here was her chance. Just because someone looked like a weasel didn't mean anything. She was trying to be really helpful and nice. Look at how long it took to get used to a new teacher in the fall.

Mrs. Minot put a delicate hand on Winnie's shoulder and guided her into the kitchen. Clara was emptying ashes from one end of the big black stove.

"I thought I heard something!" Clara said. "So it *was* you. Now look at you, you're all over shivering!"

Mrs. Minot pulled a chair over beside the stove and steered Winnie into it. She wrapped a knitted afghan around Winnie's shoulders. A powdery smell was in the wool.

"You know that Miss Taylor has forbidden anyone to go into the maze," Mrs. Minot began. "I saw you from the upstairs hall, and I started to go out after you, but I didn't want to make a fuss and rouse the household. Don't worry, though. I won't tell Harriet Taylor that you disobeyed her orders. But you should take care about the maze. You might meet with something you wish you hadn't."

Winnie began to shiver. "Like what?" Her voice made her sound like a sick mouse.

☽

"There are spirits loose in the maze. Miss Taylor doesn't believe in such things, but I know about them."

"You do?" Something in Winnie's head warned her not to say too much.

"If you tell me why you went into the maze, I may be able to help you. The maze is a dangerous place. Miss Taylor is right about that; that's the fault of the one who made it. Do you know the path, by the way?"

There was an intensity in Mrs. Minot's question, as if she wanted to hear something in particular. "Well, it's like I said last night, the maze takes people through time, I guess," Winnie answered. "Anyway, it took me, and by accident I came here from the twentieth century. It's probably a mistake. So I went out to see if I could find a trace or something of the path again, and then I could get back home and stop bothering everyone. I really don't have any business being here, though everyone is being so nice to me." A rush of shivers ran through her again, and she clutched the afghan around her arms.

Clara had finished loading the kindling and firewood into the stove and had been standing there holding a long match and staring at Winnie. Now she bent to light the stove. A pungent curl of smoke escaped from one of the iron lids. She opened the back door. "For the draft, miss. It's warming up out-of-doors. It's going to be a fair day, that's for sure."

☀

76

"Clara, you go wake Miss Harriet," said Mrs. Minot.

"Yes, Mrs. Minot." Clara's voice sounded resigned.

"And what did you find?" Violet asked when Clara had left the room.

"Nothing at all. Just weeds and bushes and old statues. The maze that I came through was painted out on the ground. I couldn't do it the first time I tried, when I found it with my friend Harry. Then the second time I went on through, easy as pie. I just want to find that old maze and go straight back through it." She tried to sound hearty and confident.

"Do you know the shape of it?" asked Mrs. Minot. "Perhaps it's in your blood to be good at these things."

"I used to be! I don't know if I could draw it now."

"Why don't you try? I'll get some paper."

Mrs. Minot rummaged in a drawer and pulled out a piece of wrinkled stationery and a thick drawing pencil. "Can you show me?"

Winnie thought for a moment and drew a maze not much like the one at the schoolyard. "I forget what a couple of the turns are," she said, "but this is almost it."

Mrs. Minot inspected the paper, folded it up, and put it in her apron pocket. She smiled at Winnie. "You know the mazemaker, then."

"The mazemaker?"

"Yes, the person who laid it out in the first place and gave it power. That's a lost art now, or almost lost. Some people believe mazemaking is a witch's tool."

"A *witch?*"

"Well, now, there are good witches as well as bad, but there's not many left of either one, so you needn't take such a fright."

"I sure don't know any witches. They're all gone where I come from."

"Perhaps. He may not be one, for all I know."

"Who?"

"The mazemaker."

Mrs. Minot busied herself before a china cabinet, apparently counting cups and saucers and rearranging them, flicking away dust motes with a white cloth. In a moment she continued in a friendly tone. "We must try to find the maze path together. I wouldn't go off hunting for it on my own if I were you, if you really want to get back where you started. It could trap you, or take you to some other time, not your own. And you mustn't talk of this to our little friend Lily. She tells everything to her aunt. She's a bit of a chatterbox, she can't help herself. But this sort of a thing is not a subject for tattletales. It must be just between us."

"Yes," Winnie whispered. She craned her neck to see through the door Clara had left open. Beyond the threshold, the sun, fully risen, shone on swaths of green grass and blossoming flower beds. Winnie had the strange sensation that she was in the grip of winter, sitting by the fire clutching her afghan, while outside, in a real world she could no longer reach, summer and sunshine went galloping on.

"These things, these lost arts, are secrets always," Mrs. Minot went on in a soft voice. "Once many people know about them, that's when the danger comes."

Now Winnie was hot, sitting so close to the stove that had roared into full heat. But she couldn't seem to move. She thought she might be getting smaller, shrinking and shriveling like a dried apple, when with several noisy thumps Lily burst into the kitchen. "So here you are! I was looking in your room for you. Have you had breakfast? What are you doing up so early? Why didn't you get me up?"

"I—I was looking for my clothes," Winnie said. It was immediately obvious she was lying. Lily looked at her with a puzzled expression.

"I was just getting her things," Mrs. Minot said, and disappeared into the room behind the kitchen. She returned with Winnie's shorts and T-shirt, stiff and dry. "Now then, you get dressed, and Clara will fix you some breakfast."

As soon as Winnie had put on her own shorts and shirt, she started to feel like her regular self. She hoped Mrs. Minot would be gone from the kitchen when she went back down.

Fortunately she was. Clara had fixed oatmeal

☽

79

and set out a pitcher of cream. Lily had already begun eating. Winnie would have given anything for a glass of cold orange juice.

"Do you wear clothes like that all the time?" asked Lily.

"Sure. They're comfortable."

"I don't see how your mother lets you out half-dressed," said Clara.

"I'm not half-dressed—these are my complete clothes," said Winnie. "For summer," she added.

"But you'll take too much sun!" Clara said.

"I want to get tan," said Winnie.

"Oh." Clara looked skeptical. "Alfred's taking Miss Taylor early to fetch some things from the dressmaker," she went on. "She'll be back after lunch. She says you must amuse yourselves and stay out of the noonday sun. Mrs. Minot says to keep away from the house while we do some heavy cleaning in the front rooms."

When Lily and Winnie had finished, they stepped out the back door and into the bright sun. Everything smelled fresh, and it was quiet, only the sounds of birds and the wind, and some random clunks and thwacks behind the sheds— some workman doing a job. It was never this quiet at home, and it never smelled this good outside. *At home.* She'd have been gone four days now. Her mother and Lew must be sick with worry. They would have called the police. Winnie had once seen a family on a television news program who didn't know where their child was. It made her feel

☼

awful to think of her own family in such misery.

"Let's run," said Lily. "I want to see you run in those shoes."

They ran across the thick grass and down the slope toward the barn. Winnie caught a glimpse of water reflecting off to her left in the distance, and someone moved out of sight as they charged past the barn. Winnie could run a lot faster than Lily, and she reached the maze first and banged into the fence. Another rail fell off, exposing rotten wood. They stood there for a moment, and then Lily slapped at her neck. "Ugh! Mosquitoes! They're everywhere!" She turned and ran up the hill and threw herself down onto the grass. Winnie followed her, and they stretched out side by side.

"What were you really doing this morning?" Lily asked. "I could hear Mrs. Minot from upstairs, but I couldn't understand what she was saying."

"She was telling me some of those stories about the maze. She says she wants to help me get back."

"Aunt Harriet's the one that will help you."

"But how can she?"

"She can do whatever she decides to," said Lily, jumping to her feet. "I'll get some corn bread and we'll go down by the pond and have a picnic! Wait here." She hurried off.

Winnie got up from the grass and walked closer to the barn. She turned to look once more at the house. Her back was to the barn, and she could feel the sun's heat in its broad, red-painted boards.

☽

In a moment an uneasy sense grew that someone was watching her. She was getting almost too
hot, and the sun was achingly bright as it beat
against the side of the barn. The door was behind
her, its simple wooden latch out of the slot. She
pulled it open and stepped in. It was cooler inside
but pitch dark. She blinked, unable to see anything
at first. Then, to her right, she made out a ladder
leading up to a square opening in the ceiling not far
from where she stood. There seemed to be a room
at the top. She climbed up and found herself in a
large square space with a cot on one side and a
chest of drawers on the other. She turned back to
the square hole where the top of the ladder rested
and stooped to look down. Little by little her eyes
got used to the dark, and then she realized she was
looking at a person: someone was watching her
from the far wall of the barn.

CHAPTER EIGHT

CHAPTER
EIGHT
CHAPTER
EIGHT
CHAPTER
EIGHT
CHAPTER
EIGHT
CHAPTER
EIGHT
CHAPTER
EIGHT
CHAPTER
EIGHT

The figure came out of the shadows and crossed to the ladder, grasped the side, and put one heavy boot on the bottom rung. Quick as a flash, Winnie stooped over and shoved the top of the ladder away from the square opening. It clattered onto the barn floor, sending dust motes and bits of straw swirling violently in the gloom. As the figure sprawled backward, Winnie saw that it was a man, taller than she was, with a shock of dark hair and rough clothes. He regained his feet, picked up the ladder, and knocked it back into place. He stood at the bottom, steadying the ladder and staring up at Winnie. Then he began to climb. He kept climbing, slinging his weight heavily from rung to rung, a determined look in his eye. He caught Winnie's glance and held it as he advanced.

"Don't come any closer!" Winnie shrieked.

He didn't say a word but kept on climbing. Through her fright Winnie saw that his cheeks were a fresh, rosy red, and his hands and wrists looked tanned and strong. The closer he came, the younger he looked. He stepped out onto the floor of the loft and stood there, as if stricken with helplessness, his arms hanging at his sides, a good foot taller than she was. Winnie felt quaky, but she clenched her fists and curled her toes to keep herself steady.

They confronted each other in the shadowed loft. The only sound was a swoosh and a thump on the roof, as if some big bird had come to roost. Winnie's heart was beating furiously in her ears, and her face was boiling hot. He was very tall—as tall as a grown-up—and broad-shouldered, too. His eyes scanned her bare legs as if he had never seen a pair of knees. The boy reached toward Winnie with one large hand, and her fear surged up once more. She couldn't move, didn't move. There was nowhere to run. His hand came closer, and she was sure he was reaching for her throat. The hand came to rest on her shoulder, and its owner let out a long breath.

"You're not a wraith, then," he said. His voice cracked in the middle of his sentence. He removed his hand. His knees looked a little quavery, too.

"A what? A wreath?" asked Winnie indignantly.

"You're substance, that I can tell," said the boy.

"My name is Winnie Brown, and I'm not a substance, I'm a person. Who are you?"

"Thomas," said the boy.

There was a pause while they both regained their breath.

"What did you mean, I'm a substance?" she asked.

"I said substance, not *a* substance," he said. It was hard to understand him, though he spoke slowly. His words ran together, and some of them were clipped or cut short. "Not a spirit, is what I mean. Turning up in the maze like that, the way they say someone will. It's common knowledge."

"What is? Does everybody know I'm here?"

"It's common knowledge the maze is haunted."

"Harriet Taylor doesn't seem to think so."

"No, not her, but the others. Me, and the Minots, and others in the village."

"Haunted?"

"Yes. They say a woman walks the maze. None of us goes in there, anyhow, because of the bog."

"What about the bog?"

"Don't you know anything, girl? A bog's a bog. Pestilence and damp."

"Don't you call me 'girl'." Winnie stamped her foot.

The boy's face closed up. He stepped back and

ducked his head. "All right, miss," he said humbly.

Winnie was mortified. "No, no, I didn't mean to—to sound like that. Just call me by my name. You can call me Winnie."

"Winnie," he repeated.

Winnie sensed that she had lost him. "I didn't mean to sound unfriendly."

"Yes." He just stood there, his big hands dangling at his sides.

"Well, what are you doing out here?" she asked. "You scared me half to death, coming out of the shadows that way."

"I wanted to see for myself," he said. "I must go, then." He abruptly started down the ladder.

"You'd best come down from there. That's my room. It's none of your affair."

"But can't you tell me some more? I want to know about the maze."

When he reached the foot of the ladder, he looked up at her, no smile on his face, but a look of steadfast interest. "Do you now," he said, and turned away. Halfway across the barn floor he stooped down and picked up something and tucked it under one arm. He shoved open the heavy door and stepped out. In the rectangle of light that framed him, Winnie saw that he was carrying a cat—a white cat with patches of black and gold.

Lily came down the lawn from the house, waving a bundle wrapped in a blue napkin. "Let's go sit by the pond."

☀

"Who's that boy in the barn?" Winnie asked as they waded through the long grass.

"Were you in the barn? That's only Thomas. He's a boy who works around the place. He's so . . . I don't know! His father was awful—he was a blacksmith, dark and scowly, and spent all his life in a shed hammering on red-hot horseshoes, and Thomas—ugh. He smells like a barn."

Winnie remembered standing close to Thomas, but to her he had smelled good—of leather and straw. Her heart gave an unexpected jump in her chest.

"Do you want to know something funny?" Lily went on. "When I went back to the house, nobody was cleaning. There wasn't a sound. I couldn't find anybody. I walked down the hall looking for Clara, and I thought I heard someone in Aunt Harriet's library. So I opened the door, and there was Mrs. Minot, with all the desk drawers open, and papers spread out on the chairs and everywhere. She saw me and snapped at me— 'Didn't I tell you to stay away?'—and slammed the door right in my face."

"What was she looking at?"

"I don't know, but my aunt always locks her desk, because she doesn't want anyone going through her papers. She told me once that she keeps private letters and bank accounts and papers about Crescent Ridge in her desk. She told me so I wouldn't be so curious and want to look in myself. But she said none of it was anyone's business but her own. Mrs. Minot must have hunted around for the key and opened the desk when she thought no one was here. Don't you think I should tell Aunt Harriet?"

"Yes, you better."

"I found Clara in the cellar. She said Mrs. Minot told her to sort out jelly jars, though it's nowhere near jelly-making season, and Mrs. Minot knows Clara hates the cellar. There are spiders down there, and it's awfully dark."

They came over the ridge, and Lily half ran, half slid ahead, down the embankment. Winnie stopped and stared. She knew precisely where she was. Before her lay Andrews Pond, with the same outline it was to have in her own time—a long, lazy, eight shape, with two small islands in one of the loops. Winnie jogged slowly down the embankment to the water's edge. Were these pebbles the same ones that would lie on the narrow beach in a hundred years? That stone was. A large, flat boulder stuck up from the bottom of the pond, its surface above the waterline and warm in the sun. It was her favorite spot for watching water bugs.

"Come on!" Lily waved to her from farther along the shore. She had gone around a curve that Winnie had negotiated a million times on her bike. Lily patted the large root of a tree that grew partway up the slope. The root was broad and grew horizontally along the hill so that it formed a bench. *This tree isn't here anymore,* thought Winnie. *Only the stump is left, like a round table—gray and dry and ringed.*

☀

They sat side by side, and Lily pointed out to the middle of the water. "There's my island," she said.

"That's *my* island!" said Winnie. "It looks just this way at home. Only there's a huge old willow tree with branches that bend down to the water."

"Then it's going to be *our* island," said Lily. "And look back there." She turned and pointed over her shoulder to the big house in the distance. "The watchdog!" A small, erect figure in a dark dress stood and watched them from the porch. At first Winnie thought it was Aunt Harriet, home early from the dressmaker, but then she saw that it was Mrs. Minot, just standing and looking, as still as anything.

CHAPTER NINE

CHAPTER
NINE

CHAPTER
NINE

CHAPTER
NINE

CHAPTER
NINE

CHAPTER
NINE

CHAPTER
NINE

CHAPTER
NINE

"You girls must rest during the heat of the day," Mrs. Minot told them after lunch. She had given them lettuce and leftover roast lamb, thin gray slices edged with crescents of fat. She seemed indifferent to Winnie, as if she had no special interest in her. "Go to your rooms now, or you'll forget yourselves and run around. Miss Taylor said to be sure you didn't get exhausted. Lily isn't used to constant company. And no more snooping! Are you listening, Lily Taylor? Miss Harriet asked me to sort out some papers for her before her trip, and she wanted it done in private."

"*I* wasn't the one snooping!" exclaimed Lily. She looked as if she was about to say something else, but thought better of it. "Can we take our rest in the old sun room? There are three daybeds, and we don't care if they're dusty."

"It's right overhead, so if I hear you walking about, I'll come up and that will be that. They aren't dusty, either. Clara's been up there lately."

Up on the second floor, at the end of a short corridor Winnie hadn't seen before, Lily opened a pair of curtained glass doors. A blast of hot air hit them. They pushed open windows on all three sides, and soon a breeze carried in the smell of cut grass and roses. Lily lay down on one couch, and Winnie on another, a hard, narrow wicker chaise longue next to a window.

"Let's pretend we're asleep," said Lily. In a few minutes genuine snores rose from the brown cushions.

Winnie propped herself up on one elbow and looked out. A bumblebee buzzed louder and louder and then flew right into the room over her head. Guess screens haven't been invented yet, she thought. She was never going to get to sleep. She hadn't taken a nap since she was three years old.

She turned on one side, trying to find a comfortable position on the hard cushion. What she really wanted to do was get another look at that cat.

Winnie picked up her sneakers and slowly crossed the sun porch on bare feet. Without a squeak she found her way down the corridor to the top of the back stairs. A rhythmic thump, thump, thump was coming from the kitchen. Winnie tiptoed down the stairs far enough to peek. Clara was

☽

at the far end of the kitchen, ironing.

"Excuse me," said Winnie. "Could I have a drink of water?"

"I don't mind," said Clara. She set the iron on the woodstove to reheat it and filled a dipper with water from a big bucket beside the sink. It was delicious. Winnie had never thought of water as tasting like anything.

"Do you mind if I sit here?"

"All right," said Clara. She turned her back and continued pressing a large white tablecloth.

"Do you think I'm a ghost, too?" Winnie asked.

"Don't know," said Clara, turning partway around. She picked up the billowing cloth and folded its snowy width in half, caught it, folded it again. There was a sweet smell in the room, a compound of hot iron and damp cloth and starch. "There's strange things going on, strange doings, and it has been so for days now. First William disappears; and then you come, and that was peculiar, you just lying out there on the grass from nowhere. And Miss Harriet's so upset on account of William being gone, or murdered, we don't know, and even Mrs. Minot is not her usual self."

"William was murdered?"

"What else could have happened? Murder! There's cutthroats in the countryside. Even going along the road to the village, if you come up against one, what's to stop him from slitting your throat? Of course, she doesn't want to say so, with Lily so easily upset."

☀

92

"If he got murdered on the road, wouldn't someone find him?"

"They could hide his body in a ditch. Or carry it away on a wagon, and he'd never be seen again. And then will Miss Harriet be grieving! It'll be the end of everything. Everything!"

"Well, maybe it didn't happen."

"Miss Harriet is so fond of William—anyone can see it—she'll go to pieces if they don't find him. He's handsome—you'd need a heart of stone not to see that. She's in love with him, even though she's older. She's twenty-nine, you know. Whatever he says to do, however he wants it done, she follows his directions. He practically runs the place. He has spirit to him, he attracts folks. Though there's some in the village that don't like him. To think of him dead, gone, murdered!" She began to cry.

Winnie got up and gingerly patted Clara on the back. "You shouldn't get so upset until you know for sure."

"It's my spells. I get crying spells, and there's nothing I can do."

"Probably you're just getting it out of your system." That was something Mrs. Austin would say.

"Getting what out?" bawled Clara. "My mother used to say she had the remedy for the spells, but she's been gone since last year, and I've no one to tell me."

So Clara was an orphan, and had to be a servant on top of it. She looked like she was sixteen or seventeen now, but probably she'd had to start

☽

working when she was much younger. Winnie would hate it if she had to go to work ironing and washing and serving soup next year, instead of going on to eighth grade. Eighth grade—if only she got there! She'd baby-sit for Daisy, clear the table, load the dishwasher, even scrub the bathroom. She'd do anything, but she had to get back home.

Before she knew it, her own face had puffed up, tears flooded her eyes, and her nose began to sting. She stood there and cried with Clara. After a moment Clara gave her a gentle pat on the arm. "There, there, don't you cry, lamb, we'll see that you get home! It must be terrible missing your mother and father. You're a brave girl, and we'll all help, just you wait and see. Take this." She handed Winnie one of a stack of beautifully ironed hand-kerchiefs. Winnie blew her nose and felt better.

"I think I'll go out and get some fresh air," said Winnie. "Is that fellow Thomas outside?"

"Don't know. You can always try the barn." Clara turned back to her ironing with a few last sniffs.

Winnie slipped out of the house and walked down the slope to the maze fence. The tangle of shrubs seemed repellent, as if it would push her even farther away if it could. She walked over to the back of the barn, hoping to see either Thomas or the cat. "Hello?" she called through a crack in the boards. "Thomas?" The heat was stifling. Sweat ran down the side of her face. There were all sorts of places where he could be, and she didn't know any of them.

☼

94

She slipped around to the big barn door, pulled it open, and stepped in. It was even hotter inside. The barn was enormous, at least three stories high, with a huge loft and great empty stalls littered with dirty straw. A large bird flew around high up near the roof, its wings flapping heavily. "Thomas?" Winnie called up toward the loft. The barn door banged open.

"What? Who's there?" Thomas stood outside, peering into the dusty darkness.

"Just me, Winnie."

"What do you want?"

"I need to ask you something."

"Then come out here where there's air. The barn's hot as an oven in midday." He led her to an apron of shade beneath a tree.

"You know that cat in the barn? Is it yours?"

Thomas was silent for a minute, and then he said, "It's William's cat."

Winnie shivered in spite of the heat. "William— the one who disappeared? What do you think happened to him?"

"Why should I know?" he said. His voice cracked, perhaps with worry.

"Lily's aunt said you are his helper."

"Yes, he taught me near everything I know."

"Is he older than you?"

"A few years. I'm sixteen. He's never said how old he is."

"I'm twelve. I'm pretty close to thirteen."

"You're younger than Lily, but you look older."

☽

Winnie nodded. She glanced at his hands: he had large, sturdy, suntanned knuckles with a scattering of freckles.

"There's the cat yonder!" Thomas jumped up and pointed to a patch of Queen Anne's lace. The cat was leaping and pawing at the bouncing, lacy flower heads. "Here, puss!" In a moment Thomas had her captured. He let her down beside Winnie, who reached out and rubbed her head and back. The cat curled up next to Winnie's foot. "Hi, Tab," Winnie said softly.

"She knows you," Thomas said.

"You remember when you told me that people in the village say the maze is haunted?" Winnie asked. "You thought it was me doing the haunting, didn't you?"

"I didn't know. Maybe."

"You don't still think I'm a ghost now, do you?"

"No!" He gave a friendly laugh. "But there's something strange about you all the same. It's your clothes, of course, but that's not all. You're not like us."

"I'll tell you what it is. I did come through the maze, but I wasn't haunting it. The maze carries you through time. It brought me back a hundred years. I really live in 1989, not 1889."

"Lord," breathed Thomas. "So it works, after all."

"I can't get back now. The path is gone."

"But there is a path—that's what people say. They say it's just as well it's hidden, maybe gone

✺

forever, because it stirs evil longings. It leads to another world."

"Ugh," said Winnie. "It was this cat that gave me the idea. Hey, puss, do you have evil longings? She went around the maze, and then I tried it the next day. My friend Harry was there, too. I was hoping he'd come through, not just me." She was beginning to feel Harry's absence a little less acutely. It was nice just sitting here with Thomas and nobody else. She felt quite a bit older, like fifteen. "So I guess the cat knows more than we do," Winnie said lightly.

"This cat goes about her own business," said Thomas. "William told me to look out for her when he was away. He said let her go her own way, and don't confine her. She hunts at night."

If only cats could talk. Tab's eyes flickered at Winnie with no more interest than if she had been a telephone pole. Cats were always distant, thought Winnie, nothing like dogs, which jumped on you in a friendly way and licked your knees.

"Did William say he was going away?" asked Winnie. "Did he say that before he disappeared?"

Thomas gave a half shrug, which could have meant yes and could have meant no.

"Did William know about the maze?"

"I gave my word I'd not say anything," Thomas answered carefully, but his expression plainly said yes.

A comfortable silence grew between them. They were sitting so close to each other, Winnie wondered what it would be like if Thomas kissed

☽

her. She had always wondered about that, what it was like when people kissed each other and if they really liked it, but this was the first time the thought had throbbed with more than curiosity. She didn't want him to, though, and he didn't.

On sudden inspiration Winnie jumped to her feet. She scooped up the cat. "Come on, Tab, let's see if you can still find the maze!" She carried Tab over to the gate and dumped her inside the fence. With a meow of protest the cat slipped back under the bottom rail and scampered away.

"You can't get her to do what she hasn't a mind to," said Thomas.

"I guess not. I never heard of cats liking mazes, anyway. I thought it was only rats in laboratories."

"How's that?"

"Nothing. I'm supposed to be taking a nap. I forgot." Winnie looked back up at the house. "Lily will wonder where I am if she wakes up. Goodbye!" Winnie ran back to the house and tiptoed up to the sun porch. She found no one there. Lily was sitting primly in the front parlor, a book in her lap, looking mad as hops.

"I see you're getting awfully friendly with Thomas," she said. Her voice was sharp with contempt. "What were you talking about?"

"Were you spying on me?"

"Not spying. You woke me up when you crept out of the sun porch, and I watched you from the window. I don't see how you can bear him."

☼

98

"What's wrong with him?"

"He's common. He scarcely knows how to read! Don't you have any sense about these things? Or maybe in your family you don't care about whether you're fine or not."

"I guess we don't!" Winnie said. "Someone who's your friend is your friend. It doesn't matter about whether they can read." Come to think of it, though, she didn't know anyone who couldn't read.

"It matters here."

"Well, it shouldn't!"

"Pooh!"

They sizzled in silence for a moment. "What were you talking about?" Lily asked again.

"The maze. And William's cat. See, I'm sure that's the cat that went through the maze ahead of me."

"What did he say about that?"

"He said that the village people know there's some old path there, and it's supposed to be evil."

"Evil?" said Lily. "I don't see how a maze can be evil, if all it does is go back in time."

"Right."

"Look. Once Aunt Harriet's gone away, we can go in the maze all we want to. We're going to find that path, no matter what."

"I forgot that she's going away."

"Don't worry. Mrs. Minot will take care of us while she's gone."

CHAPTER TEN

When Aunt Harriet returned from her errands later that afternoon, she promised them they could row out on the pond the next day. There was still time before dinner, so Lily got out her badminton set, and she and Winnie put up the net in the yard. The birdies had real feathers, not plastic ones. Winnie was usually terrible at sports, and Lily, even wearing skirts, was much better than Winnie. She won every time. Winnie was soon exhausted, and too tired to eat much of the chicken Clara had roasted for their supper. She went up to her room before it was completely dark.

She climbed into bed, but as soon as she had pulled up the sheet, she wasn't sleepy anymore.

She got up to prop open the window, shut by Mrs. Minot, and a fresh breeze blew in. Everything smelled so good. At home during the summer she smelled smoky asphalt where roads were being repaired, or exhaust fumes from traffic, or, on very hot days, the terrible stink of the garbage dumpster in back of Zinger's supermarket. "That's the city for you," Lew would say cheerfully. At night it was never quiet, never really dark. Crescent Ridge reminded her of a summer at her grandparents' house long ago. They were her father's parents, and they had invited her to come by herself to stay with them for a week when she was nine. That was before her mother had even met Lew, much less married him. She had gone alone on a bus, and although she had wanted to go, she had been scared to death of what they would be like, and wondered what she could say to them or how she should act.

Their house had a sad feeling about it, though they had been very kind to her: kind but distant. They had had acres of green woods and meadows around them, and a shaded brook, and a treehouse that her grandfather told her he had built the year she was born.

They had mostly watched her. Winnie thought she had never been so looked at in her life; and she had been good the whole time. Once they had offered to show her pictures of her father when he was a boy, but she had politely refused, because at home her mother had been so adamant about putting pictures of him away. Winnie had realized immediately that she had bewildered her grandpar-

☽

ents by saying no, and she only compounded the injury by adding, in a prim, good-girl's voice, that her mother had said they must not dwell on the past. For the next two days she squirmed unbearably in silence, trying to make herself retract her words, trying to get up the courage to ask to see the pictures, after all. They had put the three scrapbooks back into a heavy drawer in the dining-room sideboard, and so there was no way she could just sit down and pick them up and look at them. *Ask me again*, she had silently begged, but mental telepathy didn't work in Illinois.

The night before she was to go home, she had been sitting on the back stoop, swatting mosquitoes. She was staring across at the dark masses of lilacs that swept down and across the land behind the house, when a brilliant greenish light had flashed so quickly that she thought she was imagining things. Then another flash came, in another corner of the field below the house, and as soon as she turned her head in that direction, she thought she saw another out of the corner of her eye. Then there was no mistaking them: so many began to shine and wink that the night took on a magical look, thousands of lights, all silent, sparking and glowing, and in the background a solitary bird sang once or twice.

Her Grandmother Brown had come up behind her and was standing there watching, too. "Birds don't often sing at night," she had said.

Winnie had been in such a turmoil about leaving the next day, not sure that her grandparents wanted her there, anyway, and feeling generally uncomfortable, that she had been unable to respond. The silence stretched out over several minutes, and finally her grandmother had turned away and gone inside the house. In a while the fireflies had stopped flashing, and Winnie had gone up to bed. The next day she left. "Thank you for letting me come," she had said to them at the bus station, heeding her mother's insistent advice to mind her manners.

"Good-bye, then," her grandfather said, and she had boarded the bus and ridden away in a noisy roar that drowned out the voices of passengers, the cars around the station, the turnpike traffic, and finally the uncomfortable memory of herself there, wishing she had acted differently. She had thought they would never invite her back; and sure enough, on her next birthday they sent her a card and a ten-dollar bill but no note, no invitation. Now it was impossible to see them. She wondered if she would ever get another chance, or if they would even be alive by the time she got back.

The next day, the weather was particularly fine. Aunt Harriet announced that she was going to leave on her trip early in the afternoon. Alfred would drive her to the train station, and Winnie and Lily were supposed to be back in time for her departure. Clara had packed them a picnic lunch. They put it in the bow of the rowboat, and Winnie and Lily climbed in and sat together, their feet on either side of the basket. Thomas took off his boots and rolled up his pants and waded in, pushing the boat farther into the water. He climbed in, tilting everything so they squealed, and pushed away. Birds wheeled over their heads, calling and crying, and Winnie felt a surge of hope as they moved out onto the water: she loved the dip of the oars, the lapping of waves, the breeze drifting through her hair. Thomas rowed effortlessly, his arms strong and sure. Winnie leaned over and trailed a hand through the water. It made a rippled path, the lines spreading out into a gentle fan and then dissolving into the moving mirror of the water.

"How long will Aunt Harriet be gone?" asked Winnie.

"Four or five days," said Lily. "Plenty of time for—" She glanced at Thomas and stopped.

"You can say it. He knows," said Winnie.

There was an awkward silence.

"Thomas knows I have to find the maze." Nobody said anything. "She'll help, too," said Winnie to Thomas. "Well, look, I've got to have both of you or I'm really stuck." Neither of them said anything or looked at the other.

"I wish Aunt Harriet wasn't going away," said Winnie. "Mrs. Minot makes me nervous."

"We'll stay away from her," said Lily. "She doesn't really like anyone except Aunt Harriet. She wouldn't care two sticks for me if I wasn't Aunt Harriet's niece."

"What about William? Clara said everyone was fond of William."

☀

"Mrs. Minot's afraid of William," said Thomas abruptly.

"Afraid? How do you know?" asked Lily.

"From seeing with my own eyes."

"Why would she be afraid of him? How could anyone be afraid of him? He's very shy, and his speech is strange, to tell you the truth, but he's handsome. You should see him, Winnie!"

"Clara says Aunt Harriet is in love with him," said Winnie.

"In love with him!" said Lily, sitting bolt upright and rocking the boat. "She needs him to run Crescent Ridge, but she can't be in *love* with him. My parents say Aunt Harriet is almost too old to get married. Once she was engaged for three years, but she broke the engagement. Mother still hopes she'll find someone suitable who's older. William's not suitable, and he's not older, either."

"Why isn't he suitable?" asked Winnie.

"Well, he has no family. Nobody knows where he came from. He told Aunt Harriet he had escaped with his life, and he refused to say anything more."

"You know what else Clara told me? She's afraid William got murdered," said Winnie. "She says Aunt Harriet thinks so, too, but she doesn't want to say it."

"Not murdered!" breathed Lily.

They fell silent. Thomas struggled to row them across a band of currents.

"Why don't we have our picnic over there?" Lily pointed to a tiny cove on the side of the island.

☽

105

When the boat scraped the rocky bottom, Lily and Winnie strung their shoes around their necks and picked up the basket and waded ashore.

"I'll tie up farther around the bend," Thomas called to them.

The water was freezing cold and washed in thin waves over Winnie's feet. She could see the smooth rocks beneath, yellow and brown and slippery with fine moss. Her feet were stinging from the cold by the time she reached the bank. The grass there was long and warmed by the sun.

"Let's spread the blanket out here," said Winnie. She and Lily flapped it open and laid it down, pinning one corner with the picnic basket.

Thomas waded up the shoreline. "It's a fine day now, for sure," he said.

"Let's go for a walk," said Lily, jumping up and brushing off twigs and bits of grass.

The three climbed a little rise that gave a view across the pond. In the distance Winnie could see the white house and a tiny figure in a blue dress walking around the back garden: Clara hanging out the wash. In the other direction stretched a woods, and in between lay meadows and an orchard. Winnie tried to place the Moloney Spa and Pepp's Pizza somewhere on the green hills, but she couldn't picture where the street was, or the parking meters, or the purple streetlights at night, or the Styrofoam hamburger cartons crushed in the gutter.

On the other side of the hill, up a scrubby slope, they found wild strawberries, tiny and plump and tart-sweet. Winnie popped one in her mouth and felt her cheeks ache with the rush of flavor. She gathered a handful and tried to eat them slowly, one by one; she couldn't resist letting the last ten fall into her mouth all at once.

They moved along without talking. Winnie followed the shoreline, sometimes stooping down to watch a school of minnows dart up toward the bank and swerve away. She could hear a frog croak, and then with a splash it would leap to safety as she walked along. It was always quicker than she was. It would croak again, farther down; or else it was a different frog. The sun warmed her back as she crouched down to study a rock in a shallow puddle. A small green turtle sunned itself under her gaze.

If she found the maze path, not only could she go back home, she could make return visits. She could come back here whenever she wanted to. She could bring people with her. Harry would like this, especially if he knew he could get out again. Even Daisy would. She could lie on her blanket and wave her fists around in the shade of that apple tree. Little green knobs, the beginnings of apples, decorated the branches among the leaves.

For that matter, if she could go back and forth, she could change a few things in the past. She might try out all sorts of harmless plans that could produce interesting results in her own time.

They had worked their way around the whole island by now and were back to the blanket.

☽

Thomas threw himself down on the grass. He lay on his back with his hands behind his head. Winnie lay on her stomach, half on the blanket, but with her elbows resting in the grass so she could look down into it. At home she used to like to push aside blades of grass and watch the insects run. She would pretend they were natives in a foreign jungle and she was playing sun god, piercing their shadowy world with the light of day. The game didn't seem so interesting now.

"What's it like in 1989?" asked Lily. "Crescent Ridge is still here, isn't it?"

Winnie pictured the nursing home with its rows of chairs and aluminum awnings. "It's there, but it doesn't look the same. Everything is different. There are streets all around here, and every place is packed with houses. There aren't any big fields. The pond's still the same, though."

"Who lives at Crescent Ridge? Do I live there?" Lily laughed nervously. "No, I'd be too old. A hundred and thirteen. Guess I'm dead." She laughed again.

"I don't know the people there," said Winnie carefully.

"What is it like? Tell everything about it."

It was hard to know where to begin. "Some things we have, you have, too. Like, I saw a picture explaining a vacuum cleaner in one of Aunt Harriet's magazines. Everyone has those at home, they're nothing special. And we have other things you probably can't imagine. We have lights everywhere. You flick a switch in the wall and a light bulb comes on. In the cities there are incredibly tall buildings, all lit up and glittering at night, and cars going by with headlights, and even signs flashing with lights. We have airplanes, huge machines that people fly in, sort of like a train. People fly to France in a few hours."

"Are you making this up?" asked Lily.

"We wear shorter clothes. There are shots you get to keep you from getting diseases."

"No one gets sick?" asked Thomas.

"People do, but not with certain things, like smallpox. There's medicine to make you get well. And computers—" She stopped. She kept thinking of machines and inventions, but that didn't explain why her time felt so different from theirs. "And we've had men go to the moon. Really stand right on it. They went in a rocket ship," she finished.

Thomas snorted. "What did they do that for?"

"I wish I could go into the future," said Lily. "Except I wouldn't go unless I was sure Winnie would be there."

"But you don't know that the maze goes to Winnie's time," said Thomas. "What if it only runs backward? What if William went into the maze and got taken back a hundred years and he's trapped there?"

"Then at least he wouldn't be murdered!" Lily said.

Winnie swallowed. "You think the maze always goes backward? Did anyone tell you that?"

☽

Lily and Thomas looked at Winnie, hearing the urgency in her voice.

"Do you know that for sure?" Winnie asked.

Thomas shook his head. "No—not for sure. I was only trying to figure it out."

"Is anybody hungry?" said Lily. They had forgotten about lunch. There was half a roast chicken, left from the night before, a new loaf of bread, some farmer's cheese, a pot of jam, and some apples that had been stored all winter and were sweet and mealy. There was a slice of white cake that Lily broke into three fairly even pieces. After a moment's hesitation she gave the largest to Thomas.

After they had finished eating, they all lay on their stomachs in the sun. Winnie drifted in and out of sleep, now jerking awake, thinking she was home again; now dreaming that she was running through the tangled garden maze, pushing through dark branches to reach the silver center that shone just one more turn away. Then she was there, but it turned out she was standing in the center of a vast desert of gray asphalt. She ran back out, cutting across curving painted lines to the outermost rim of the schoolyard, only to find when she turned that she stood in the woods again, and deep in the darkness ahead gleamed the silver turns of the maze.

It was some time later when they collected themselves, folded up the blanket, and walked around to the boat. The ride across the water was swift—a northwest wind blew waves into the surface of the pond and carried them on its current. As they drew closer, Winnie saw Clara in her blue dress moving back and forth across the shoreline, and as they scraped to a halt in shallow water she ran to meet them.

"Hurry and say good-bye to Miss Harriet! She says you've been gone far too long!"

Lily ran ahead, and Thomas stayed to tie the boat securely. As Winnie came across the slope her eye was caught by a tiny patch of color on the ground, like finding an Easter egg. She stopped suddenly. There in the grass lay a toy, a small purple calico mouse, slightly chewed. She knew even before she had lifted it to her nose what it would smell like. She shoved it into her pocket and ran the rest of the way.

CHAPTER ELEVEN

CHAPTER ELEVEN
CHAPTER ELEVEN
CHAPTER ELEVEN
CHAPTER ELEVEN
CHAPTER ELEVEN
CHAPTER ELEVEN
CHAPTER ELEVEN

Aunt Harriet was waiting for them on the front steps, surrounded by pieces of luggage.

"Do you think you'll bring William back with you?" asked Lily.

"I only wish I could. Someone at the Greenwood place reported seeing a man who looked like William about a week ago. I shall never give up until I find him, you know."

Lily hugged her around the waist.

Winnie and Lily followed Aunt Harriet and the Minots out to the carriage. Alfred loaded on the suitcases. As Aunt Harriet was about to step up, she turned to Lily and Winnie. "There's something that has been on my mind, and I've decided to tell you before I go. My trip to the village left me uneasy. People I've known for years barely nodded to me on the street, though I noticed them watching me wherever I went. There are rumors about Crescent Ridge—that some sort of bad magic has taken over here. The villagers are superstitious, and they always love to talk. Mrs. Porter, the seamstress, told me they believe some curse has come back to life on our land. It's that maze again. We should have had the whole thing dug up or burned years ago. When I get back next week, I shall do that. In the meantime stay away from the maze, and stay away from the village, too. I wouldn't want you to encounter anything unpleasant.''

Alfred helped Aunt Harriet step into the carriage and settle herself, and then he climbed into the driver's seat. The carriage and sturdy horse descended the circular driveway and dwindled in the distance. Winnie and Lily ran to the crest of the hill and waved as long as they could. The noise of the clopping hoofs and squeaking wheels reached Winnie's ears long after the carriage was lost to view down the winding road. Even though Aunt Harriet talked about digging up the maze, Winnie couldn't help wishing that instead of disappearing into the distance, the carriage was coming closer and bringing Aunt Harriet home. She reached into her pocket and closed her hand around the toy mouse.

By six o'clock the heat of the day had gone, and a cold wind blew across the top of the ridge. "The wind can change like that," said Clara. The kitchen was warm with the wood stove going, and something smelled delicious. Mrs. Minot had told Lily and Winnie that they would have their supper in the kitchen—no use setting up the dining room for two children, was there? She and Alfred would eat with them, too, and Clara. Thomas would have his supper later.

Clara was chatting aimlessly as she stirred the vegetable soup that was to be their supper; Lily was licking applesauce cake batter off her fingers. A kind of unwilling comfort settled into Winnie's bones.

Clara set plates and bowls and big napkins on the table. She ladled the steaming soup into the bowls and set out a board with a cut loaf of bread on it. The Minots came in from their apartment, and Winnie squeezed into the chair next to Lily. Alfred muttered grace.

"I showed Winnie my island today," said Lily.

"Would it surprise you to know that I, too, think of it as my island?" said Mrs. Minot.

"Yours?" said Lily.

"Yes."

"Why ever do you think that?"

"It nearly was. All of Crescent Ridge nearly was mine, or my family's."

"Now, Violet, are you starting on that again?" said Alfred.

"I never heard anything about this," said Lily. "I might have been the mistress of Crescent Ridge, and you, my dear, would not be here at all!"

Lily giggled nervously. "When did all this happen?"

"A long time ago. A hundred and fifty years or more."

"And you still think about it?"

"Every day I think about it."

Lily giggled again. Winnie's heart began to beat uncomfortably fast.

"What happened?"

"My family was among the earliest settlers in this region. And shortly after they came over, they sent back to England for an orphan cousin to help clear the land and farm it. He became the father's favorite when he'd been here only a little while, and the father—that was my great-great-grandfather—said this cousin was more deserving to be his heir than his own two sons. The cousin had charmed him, put a spell on him, and charmed everyone else, too. Most probably he was a witch. There's no denying there is witching in the family.

"So the cousin made the two sons resentful, naturally. That was part of his plan. Then the cousin ran away and made it appear that the two sons had killed him. They had plenty of reason to—they were afraid their father was going to leave everything to him and skip over them. In those days it was easier to murder someone and not get caught. Nobody ever found the cousin's body, though.

☽

"The two sons' reputations were ruined after that. No one trusted them. At last they were driven into drink and carelessness. They were forever saying they hadn't done a thing, and folk got tired of hearing that and came to believe the opposite."

"What do you think?" Winnie asked.

"I'm sure they didn't kill him." Mrs. Minot's voice rang out with indignation. Winnie lowered her eyes and stared at a spot in the center of the table.

"And if their reputations had not been ruined, they would have prospered, and they'd not have lost this land. It was all sold, you see, and through the years it changed hands several times. But my ancestors stayed round about these parts and kept working for each new owner. We were all drawn to the land."

Winnie tried to imagine herself being drawn to her yard at home, but she couldn't picture it except for the attraction of the ice-cream store. Her family, though, that was different. This time of day made her feel the worst. A lonely feeling crept into her chest.

"If the cousin wasn't murdered, what did happen to him?" asked Lily.

Mrs. Minot looked at Winnie and Lily, as if she were assessing whether it was wise to tell them. "This cousin had laid out a maze in a corner field—dug it as shallow trenches, wide enough to run through. And it was there that he disappeared."

☀

Something in Mrs. Minot's voice had changed. Winnie vividly saw the dark acre with the dirt paths winding through the field grass, and a young man running for his life.

"You mean—our maze?" Lily whispered.

"Yes, our maze."

"So that's what the trenches were that my grandparents found?"

"Exactly. My Great-aunt Sally said it was a mizmaze they had found. She said in the old days, in England, they were common in country villages, and the people used them for May dances. She said this one had an enchantment on it, that it was a living thing and had powers to affect human beings, and I was to take care when I went in that I always turned to the right—never to the left, always to the right—and the power would never harm me.

"All of us children teased her for believing such a thing, but even then, at the very beginning, there were odd happenings. My Aunt Alice and Uncle Daniel took me more than once—I lived with them when I was very young because my parents were dead—and you could hear voices at certain turns, not children's voices. Then the two boys I knew went into the maze and they never came out. Must have turned left, says Aunt Sally. Other people said they had to have drowned in the pool, but no one ever found their bodies.

"The Taylors closed the maze after that, and later on that same summer, when they advertised for a servant girl, I was given the position. I was nine years old, just a little bit of a thing, but I had to work. I wanted to be here, for I always believed Aunt Sally, even though some people said she was a crazy old coot. I used to go out and look over the fence and wish I dared go in. Aunt Sally told me it was dangerous to meddle with the maze, but if anyone got hold of its power, they would be able to change around anything to suit themselves."

It was silent in the kitchen, except for the rustle of starched cloth as Clara took off her apron. Mrs. Minot looked at Winnie with steady eyes. Winnie felt overwhelmed with tiredness, as if some part of her mind were simply turning away from this, no matter what she could do. "You—you must think I know all about it, then," she said.

"I did wonder, yes."

A log shifted in the stove with a soft explosion of sparks. "Now, don't pester the girl with your crazy notions," said Alfred. "She's got no one here, she's all alone."

"I only want to help. She doesn't want to have the curse of this maze clinging to her for the rest of her life. She wants to be rid of it and go home."

Winnie was seized by an enormous yawn. Must be lack of sleep. The story, and even her own predicament, seemed distant and unimportant. If she just relaxed, everything would work out. In fact, Winnie felt so comfortable in the fragrant kitchen that she had the peculiar thought of wondering if she would still miss her family after a

☀

decent interval. Their faces bobbed like cameos in her mind, silently scolding and exhorting her to come back, to return to her own time. Daisy squalled, and Winnie was glad she wasn't there to hear her.

"How about some tea?" said Alfred.

Mrs. Minot obliged, and in a few minutes Winnie, too, had before her a huge cup of strong tea with milk and sugar stirred into it. She took several swallows and woke up. Her sense of sleepy comfort fled. Cold drafts blew through the window, but the fire in the stove lent a steady warmth to the room. Mrs. Minot lit two lamps. The big wooden table shone in the yellow light. Winnie looked out. The western sky was still pale, but deep shadows had closed around the barn, the sheds, the sweep of grass, the bulk of dark woods at the edge of the lawn, the woods that held the maze. She caught a glimpse of something—a white glow moving through the grass by the maze; then it was gone.

"I've never heard that before," whispered Lily. She sat on the edge of Winnie's bed in her night-gown. "Mrs. Minot sounded so . . . sour! Imagine her thinking she could be the mistress of Crescent Ridge! She seems different this time with Aunt Harriet gone. But we don't have to care. We'll try the maze tomorrow, just ourselves. They can't keep us out of there unless they lock us in our rooms. And they can't do that, because there aren't

☽

any locks!" Lily tiptoed from the room and shut the door behind her.

Winnie stretched out beneath the covers, her legs and arms tense with alertness. She had already decided she was not going to wait, not even till tomorrow. She was going to find her way to the center of the maze and the exact spot where she had come through. Then she would try to reverse directions and look for the path as she came out. Possibly she could reconstruct the shape of the schoolyard maze; if rats could remember a maze, so could she. She would have several hours if no one discovered she was gone. She had hidden the calico mouse under her pillow, and she reached up now and then to make sure it was still there. She was pretty sure that Harry had still had the mouse when she went around the schoolyard maze. So Tab must have gone back to get it. And that meant the maze still led to her own time.

She slipped from her bed and knelt by the window. Green dust cloaked the landscape; trees lengthened into their own shadows; a small yellow light winked in the far wing where the Minots had their quarters, and there, past the barn, she could make out the black, rounded shape of the woods. A three-quarter moon had risen well into the sky. She heard soft footsteps on the back staircase, over her head—that would be Clara going to her room over the kitchen. Winnie put on her sneakers and got back into bed and waited.

In twenty minutes the only light left in the sky was a band of blue, dotted with one bright star.

Winnie crept from her bed, took the folded quilt from the bottom drawer of the chest, unfolded it, and rerolled it into a long shape. She tucked that into her bed. She opened the door and moved slowly down the hall. The boards cracked, nothing more than they would do by themselves. The house was still—the stillness was deep on every side. She eased down the narrow kitchen stairs, crossed the kitchen in six long strides, undid the back door latch, and let herself out onto the stone stoop. The night landscape lay before her, an easy, downward slope. The wind brushed the grass. She heard frogs. It would never do to wait for the right moment. She began to walk quickly across the grass; then sudden fear gripped her and she couldn't help running. No sound came from her shoes, and she held her breath with ferocious strength. Past the barn, she let it out, gasped several times, looked behind her—the same moon-lit swath, indifferent and unknowing—nobody there. She ran for the broken gate. She climbed up and over, dropping onto the mossy ground.

The worst was past. She would not get caught.

By moonlight the woods, which looked so solid from her window, now separated itself into single trees, space into which the moon fell, and clutters of underbrush. There was thick scrub everywhere, and mosquitoes whined and swarmed like a net over the bushes. They must have smelled her coming. She plunged through the bushes, trying to ignore the thorns digging into her legs. What if she couldn't find the center? Fear began to hum as loudly in her ears as the mosquitoes. She pushed and scrabbled forward, heedless of the noise she made. A white shape formed itself before her—the statue of the woman. Was it where it had been? She thought it had faced the other way when she saw it in daylight. She ducked in front of it, turned halfway around, and pushed off through a patch of hideous evergreens whose thick, woody branches grew out like stubborn broomsticks, shoving her back. Past them, the ground was softer underfoot, and a stagnant smell reached her nose. The frogs' song grew louder. A few more yards, shoving through a mass of silky leaves, and she burst into the clearing. There was the pond, smaller than she remembered it, and the gazebo. Only this time there was someone in the gazebo.

She was too stunned to move, or even to cry out. That was a good thing, for the figure in the shadows had not seen her. A woman was sitting on a bench wearing a veil that covered her head and shoulders. She was twisted around, holding a piece of paper up to the light of the moon, and Winnie saw that she was wearing gloves. Winnie waited, trying to breathe quietly. The figure folded the paper and stood up. Then she moved to the gazebo archway and stepped down to the ground. She began to walk slowly, not quite toward Winnie, looking at the ground and talking to herself. She passed right by, then stopped and tapped the ground with her toe. She circled the pond and tested the ground again with her foot. Then she

☀

said something and took out the paper again, shook it open, and held it up. She suddenly flung back the veil, as if to get a good look at the paper, and Winnie saw who it was. It was Violet Minot. She couldn't seem to read what was written on the paper, even with the veil thrown back, and then she must have been attacked by mosquitoes, for she slapped at her neck and her arms and finally plunged away through the thickets toward the gate. So this was the ghost in the maze.

Winnie waited until the thrashing noises had stopped before she came out of her hiding place. Mrs. Minot hadn't seen her, she was sure of that, but what if she looked into Winnie's room when she went back to the house? Winnie had thought she would have plenty of time. She went over to the stone bench and tried to remember if that was where she had come through, but now she was rattled. So Mrs. Minot was trying to find the maze path for herself. It was like some awful race. Winnie had the advantage now, she was right where the maze had to be, but the more she tried to remember the place where she had come through, the more her mind refused to yield up any memory. All her recollections skittered away, until for a few horrifying moments she couldn't even remember what Harry looked like.

The mosquitoes were whining around her neck and legs and biting everywhere they found bare flesh. She never would be able to stand still long enough to look at the ground.

☽

She began to hurry out of the woods. Some yards off, she heard twigs snapping. There were plenty of small animals prowling around at night, she knew that. When she stared into the darkness, she saw only masses of shrubs and weeds; everything could have been a lurking giant but nothing was. Yet she felt someone else's presence. That was nonsense, unless Mrs. Minot had seen her, after all, and was lying in wait for her. She took a few cautious steps. Suddenly a white blur shot out of the undergrowth and streaked by, brushing her bare ankle with its fur. She heard the shriek of a small animal and a whirling of claws somewhere behind her, but she didn't stay to watch. She ran. Straight out, plunging through branches and slapping down weeds, darting across the uneven ground, she had nearly made it when she stepped wrong, turned her ankle with a violent wrench, and fell. All her weight came down on her twisted foot, and pain shot through her leg. She screamed, "Ouch! Ow, Ow!" and rolled over.

Now she had really done it. She felt intensely thirsty, cold all over, and very far away, as if she had floated out of her physical self and was waiting, waiting, waiting for something interesting to happen.

Something did—stabs of pain. "Oof!" she groaned. She just lay there. In a minute she began to feel warmer. She tried to get up on her feet, but that was out of the question. She rocked up onto her hands and knees but could only crawl five steps. If she could move on two hands and one knee, she'd be fine, but that meant dragging her foot. She couldn't stay there all night. What if she couldn't walk tomorrow? She forced herself to creep another yard or two. Sharp sticks dug into the palms of her hands, and waves of fire radiated from her ankle. "Ow!" she half yelled.

"What's the trouble? What've you done?" said a voice over her head. It was Thomas.

Almost the entire household was awakened when Thomas carried Winnie back to her bedroom. Mrs. Minot came flying down the hall from her apartment, her bathrobe knotted around her waist, as if she had never been anywhere else this evening, and Alfred padded after her in large maroon slippers. Mrs. Minot looked at Winnie's ankle. It had already swelled up into a shapeless column in which the sharp corner of her anklebone could not be seen. Winnie glanced down once, but couldn't stand to look again.

"Can you move your foot?" asked Mrs. Minot. Winnie could manage that. "It's not broken, then. I'll bind it, to keep down the swelling. We'll put it up on a pillow, and you must sleep with it elevated. Alfred, bring me the strips of sheet from the pantry."

Lily held Winnie's hand while Mrs. Minot wound the cloth firmly around Winnie's ankle and foot. Winnie hoped it was the right thing to do. There was no health clinic nearby, no X-ray ma-

☽

125

chine, not even any aspirin or Tylenol.

"I'm causing an awful fuss," Winnie croaked when she was tucked in, all except for her foot, now lying on two cushions and sticking up in the air at the foot of the bed. "You rest well if you can," said Mrs. Minot. "Now, everyone, back to bed." She shooed them out. Then she turned to Winnie. "What were you doing outside?"

"I was . . . looking at the maze. I know I wasn't supposed to be out there, but I couldn't help it. Then I tripped and twisted my ankle, and Thomas heard me crying. He came out from the barn and helped me up."

"Well, there'll be no more sneaking out now. You've fixed yourself but good." Mrs. Minot sounded disappointed. "Here's what we will do. You may go into the maze when it is daylight, when your ankle is better, and I will come with you."

CHAPTER TWELVE

Winnie's foot throbbed and sparked with pain all night. When the pain let up, the mosquito bites on her legs and arms itched like crazy. As she scratched, she kept thinking about the cat. That white blur in the maze had been Tab, probably out on a midnight hunt, and Winnie was afraid she had missed her best chance. Maybe the cat went back and forth through time whenever she was chasing mice or other prey. But Winnie couldn't follow her around day and night, and cats were not the kind of animal you could command, like dogs. Say "Go, Tab!" to her, and she would just sit down and start cleaning her feet. There was no way you could walk up to a cat and get it to do something. Mrs.

Austin had once given her a hint about solving tricky problems. "Sideways thinking," she had called it. When you can't figure out the solution to something, let your mind wander all around the problem, but don't think straight at it. Sometimes the answer will come to you.

Sometimes.

Winnie finally fell asleep, but she kept having bad dreams. She saw the maze as a glowing, malevolent tangle, a piece of giant's jewelry lying in the woods; and every time she walked toward it, it went dark.

In the morning Mrs. Minot unwound the cloth strips, and Winnie saw that her ankle was a horrible bluish purple and shaped like a soft tomato. She wasn't going anywhere on that foot today.

Clara brought her some breakfast on a tray and afterward helped her hobble downstairs and out onto the wide front porch. Lily came to find her and dragged a bench over so that Winnie could sit on a chair and prop her foot up. No sooner had Lily sat down next to her than Mrs. Minot pushed open the window between the porch and the front room. Winnie could hear rustling sounds as Violet dusted the immaculate parlor.

"Let's go out under that tree," said Winnie. She and Lily hobbled and shuffled to get Winnie down the steps. Then Lily dragged the heavy chairs and bench over to a grassy spot overlooking the barn. They settled themselves again. Winnie started to say something, and Mrs. Minot came out with her needlework and sat down next to them.

"I should scold you about last night," she said to Winnie as she punctured her embroidery cloth with her needle. "But your ankle is punishment enough. Besides, I've something to tell you. This afternoon I shall have Alfred drive us to visit Aunt Sally."

"Your Great-aunt Sally?" asked Winnie.

"She's still alive?" said Lily. "She must be a thousand years old!"

"Over a hundred, and still alive. She lives just outside the village. She still knows about the maze and the old rumors. She has forgotten nothing. She's hard to understand, but perhaps Winnie will be able to understand her."

"I will?"

"Who knows—she may even tell you how to solve the maze. I have always thought she knew its secret. She'll speak to us, and perhaps you can understand her."

"Okay," said Winnie reluctantly, as if saying it or not made any difference.

"But Aunt Harriet said not to go to the village," said Lily. "She said something unpleasant might happen."

"We will not be going into the village—only right outside it. Besides, Lily, you don't need to come."

"I want to go along! Winnie needs me to help her walk."

"Alfred can do that." Mrs. Minot stuffed her embroidery back into a brown velvet bag and stood up. "We shall leave immediately after lunch."

☽

129

"But I could help you figure out what Aunt Sally says!"

"Only the two of us will go in to see her."

"She wants it all for herself, doesn't she!" said Lily as Violet moved away across the grass. "She wants the maze!"

"That's what I've been wanting to tell you. I saw her in the maze last night, before I twisted my ankle—she was wearing a veil and gloves and walking around in the middle, trying to find her place from a piece of paper."

"You mean, like the ghost?"

"I think she *is* the ghost. I bet she's been going out there all this time, looking for the way through."

"And she just let us all go on thinking it was a ghost. But isn't it strange she would wear a veil? Unless . . . she probably had it on to keep off the mosquitoes! So what does she want in the maze? Seems to me she'd just be scared of it."

"What if she wants to go back in time, to the beginning of the maze, and get Crescent Ridge for herself? You know all she said about how it really belonged to her? What if she went back and told that ancestor of hers that the cousin was evil, or a witch or something, and persuaded the brothers to act right and hang on to their land? Then, a couple of centuries later, here she is, owning Crescent Ridge."

"But how could she know that would happen?"

"Maybe she's got it all figured out. Remember when you said you saw her in your aunt's library

☀

130

with all those papers spread? They could have been records, whatever tells you who owned Crescent Ridge when. She probably has a grand plan."

"And she just needs to know how to get through the maze. Oh, Winnie—I don't think you should go to Great-aunt Sally's!"

"She's making me. I can't run away with my foot like this. But listen—nothing bad can happen yet, because she still doesn't know how to get through, and she thinks I can find out for her. So she's got to keep me safe."

"What if Aunt Sally really does tell you? Then Mrs. Minot will know, too."

"Maybe she'll be really hard to understand."

The wagon jolted along the dirt road, rocking in and out of ruts. Though they were moving slowly, every bounce of the wagon made Winnie's ankle throb. She sat next to Mrs. Minot and behind Alfred's broad back. Alfred was motionless, except for flicking the tip of his whip over the horse's head every once in a while. The horse could have pulled them without any driver at all.

They jogged along beside open fields, passed a farmhouse, and another, and then Alfred did stir himself to turn the horse to the right, off the main road onto a path barely wide enough for the wagon. Branches overhead made a dappled tunnel. As they moved through it, long branches nearly slapped them off their seats. They emerged onto a scrubby slope with no path. They bumped down through thick grass to a colorless, patched-together house that looked as though it would fall over if you stamped your foot. Winnie could hear a stream gurgling just beyond the house, and she saw that the porch sat on sticks and looked out over a steep bank.

"Here we are! Alfred, you get her down and wait for us here." Mrs. Minot climbed down, and Alfred heaved himself off the driver's seat and hoisted Winnie to the ground. She held on to the wagon and put a little weight on her bandaged ankle, to test it. She half hopped across the grass, leaning on Mrs. Minot's skinny arm.

Violet pushed the door open a few inches, stuck her head in the crack, and called, "Aunt Sally? Are you here? I've brought someone to meet you. We'll let ourselves in." She opened the door a little farther, until it banged against something. Winnie looked into the dark interior and wondered how they were going to get in, for the room was completely full. Tables, chairs, and bureaus were crowded against and on top of one another; between and beneath them were boxes stacked as high as Winnie's shoulder. Shelves full of papers and pots and pans and jelly jars and boots rose up into the dim corners of the ceiling. There was a smell of river damp, not unpleasant. But where was Aunt Sally?

Violet led the way, turning sideways and slipping down an aisle only partly blocked by stacks of papers. At the end, beside a little table overlooking the porch, was a deep chair, and in it sat a bundle of woolly clothes. Two small legs reached down from the skirt, and finally Winnie saw a grimacing, furrowed face beneath a frizz of white hair that seemed to inhabit a world of its own, above its owner.

"Aunt Sally, this child has come from beyond," said Mrs. Minot.

"Come here!" screeched the ancient voice. Her eyes sparked with interest, and her grimace opened into a crooked smile in which one tooth was visible. Winnie had never seen anyone this old. She made Grandma Brown look like a teenager.

"You know how you used to tell me when I was little that someone would travel through the maze? She has, and now she needs to go back but doesn't know how. You can tell her, can't you?"

"Have some candy," said the old woman. It sounded like "Schram andy," but Winnie knew what she had said. She waved a quavering, shawl-draped arm. Winnie looked behind her and saw an open barrel. Toward the bottom was a mass of yellow. She reached down and touched a thousand pieces of hard candy, stuck together. They must have been there for years. Winnie tried to pry one loose, but they were petrified.

"I can't get them out," she said.

"How old?" asked the woman.

"Twelve," said Winnie.

"Have some candy."

Winnie busied herself in the bottom of the barrel again, this time breaking a fingernail. She surfaced and said, "Thank you," hoping that would settle it.

☽

Violet stood expectantly. When no more words came from Aunt Sally, she prodded Winnie: "You tell her."

"Tell her what?"

"Tell her how you came."

Winnie repeated her story of the schoolyard. At the end of it Aunt Sally chirped, "Around!"

Violet let out her breath in exasperation. "This always happens. Some people say she's lost her mind altogether."

"Around and around!" said the old woman.

Violet's nose instantly quivered with attention. "Yes, Aunt Sally, that's it. Tell us more. You used to warn me never to turn to the left, always to the right. How can we tell this child where to turn left or right? Do you have a drawing of the maze?"

"Too many." The woman shook her head and pressed her rubbery lips together. She held up two trembling fingers.

"Too many what?" snapped Violet. "Make yourself clear, can't you?"

At that the old woman grasped the arms of her chair and pulled her chin back, and Winnie saw that she was frightened. Her lips were trying to form words, but they couldn't seem to align themselves. One arm raised itself into the air and drew some weak circles. Winnie thought it might have been a spiral. The arm dropped, then rose again and drew circles in the opposite direction. "Two!" she exclaimed, leaning forward. But did she mean "two" or "too"? Or "to"? "Extra!" she said.

✻

"You ask her," said Violet to Winnie.

"I can't find the path anymore, that's the problem," said Winnie. "Is there a way to find it? It used to be gravel, but now the gravel is gone, lost under leaves and dirt."

"Lost!" That was clear enough. Aunt Sally grinned. Winnie thought she looked happy at the idea.

"I don't think she knows," said Winnie.

"She does, and she's not telling," said Violet. "Aunt Sally, if you don't help, this child will never get back to her own family! Think of her parents! Think of how the events in history will be changed and twisted if one person is taken out of her time!"

Aunt Sally cackled. "Has to go back," she gibbered cheerfully.

"Yes, that's what I'm saying. But how?" Violet insisted crossly. "I know all about turning right and not left. But where?"

"Go right, nothing. Left, through the maze!"

"You do know, you know it all, and you're playing a game with me. To think of all I've done for you—even protecting you from the villagers. Don't think they aren't suspicious. They'd have run you out of town if it wasn't for me. Don't expect to see me the next time there's an early snow and you've no firewood!" Violet yanked on Winnie's arm. "Come on."

"Ouch! My foot!" As Winnie turned to follow Violet past the piles of junk, Aunt Sally tugged on her other arm with a cool, soft, shaking hand. "The

☽

shadow," she said urgently. "Find the shadow."

"Come along. She's only babbling," said Violet, standing in the doorway. Winnie limped out, looking back to see Aunt Sally holding up two fingers.

Alfred helped Winnie into the wagon. Mrs. Minot climbed in beside her, and they jolted slowly back up the hill. "She was only being cunning," said Violet to Winnie. "She told you what to do, I am sure of it."

When their wagon reached the top of the leafy slope, they saw the path was blocked by a number of other wagons and carts and people. The people nudged one another, and a ripple of talk spread through the crowd.

"That's her, the girl there."

"How come she looks like that?"

"What's she got on for clothes?"

"Looks don't tell a thing. It's her."

They pressed close to the wagon, and a child reached up to touch Winnie's leg. Winnie snatched herself away. "What do they want?" she cried.

"Let us talk to her, the one who came through," said a woman. "We want to hear what she believes, where she's from. Is she doing the devil's work? Maybe she's got messages for us. Ask her. Ask her, John."

"Nay, nay, not me!" A robust man with a bald, sunburned head gave a belly laugh.

"We'll not let you by till we've spoken to her," said another woman wearing an apron and hugging a thin, sour-looking child in front of her.

"There's been seers before, there's a few left now," another man said, nodding. "Like old Sally yonder. Now, what're you doing calling on her?" "Let's have it out, clear and open."

They had crowded around the edge of the wagon, and a tall, skinny man with enormous, bony hands reached out and grabbed Winnie's wrist as if he meant to drag Winnie right off the bench. "Let us hear her, what she says for herself."

"You go back there." Alfred Minot cracked the man across the knuckles with his whip. "She's no more a witch than you are, Henry Acorn. There's no witches anywhere. Now get out of our way."

Alfred started the horse. People pressed back far enough to keep their toes from being run over. "We'll come down to see her," called a woman. She was stout, and her voice rang loudly over the noise of the wagon. "If'n she won't step down to speak to us, we'll come up, all of us, to call while Miss Taylor's away. We'll come for her!"

No one followed them. Winnie looked over her shoulder and watched the cluster of people dwindle. She stole a glance at Mrs. Minot. Violet was stiff with distress, looking high over the landscape, as if she were riding the prow of a ship. Alfred was hunched again into his potato posture, as if nothing had happened.

"Could you make any sense out of what Sally said?" asked Violet.

☽

137

"Not much."

"Then you're not a mazemaker after all. There is a mazemaker, perhaps more than one, and that's who knows the workings of the maze. For a while, when I was younger, I thought I might turn out to be one. I waited for clues, I drew spiral shapes. I thought I would wake up one morning and know I was a mazemaker. And then I could run through time, I could change events. I could redo the past, fix up the future. Once I sat all night in the gazebo waiting. It was a midnight long ago." Alfred shifted his position and groaned. "Shut up, Alfred. I was very young, just fifteen, and very hopeful. I had a feeling something was going to happen, happen especially to me, that very night. So I sat and waited—it was all against the Taylors' rules, and they'd have dismissed me in a moment if they had known. They said no one was to go in the maze. I expected I would be given a sign, because, years before, I had seen those boys disappear with my own eyes. I had told everyone they fell into the pond. But I had seen something else. I was nine years old. I had been spying on them through a hedge. I was going to startle them; in fact, I thought I might catch them peeing in the bushes. They chased each other round and round the sundial, and then one of them began to disappear, starting with his shoes and going up to the knees and then his knickers, and on up to his cowlick. The other one fell down right where his brother had been, and the same thing happened to him. I stood there, unable to believe it, and I turned and ran as fast as I could, only I got lost. I couldn't find my way—I kept finding dead-end paths, hedges everywhere blocking me, and turns that went past the same benches and the same statues till I thought the statues were smiling, laughing at me. Finally I fell down and fainted, and when I woke up, some men had carried me out of the maze and onto the grass. I told them what had happened, and they said, do you mean the boys fell in the pond? And I answered yes, because I didn't know what else to say. The only thing I knew was that I had witnessed some magic.

"I watched them drag the pond that day, and I knew they wouldn't find anything. When I went home to the village that night, Aunt Sally sent for me. I had to walk down to her cottage in the dark and tell her what I had really seen. She had already guessed. She told the boys' parents that their children were probably still alive and might come back someday, but they were too upset to take her seriously."

Alfred made a hacking and hawing noise as he cleared his throat. He stirred on his seat and gave the horse a flick of the whip.

"Aunt Sally told me then that there was someone somewhere who knew the maze. In those days she made sense, you see. Someone had laid it out at another point in time and still could use it. And she said others with the same gift would come along, and maybe we ourselves would see this

꒰

mazemaker if we watched for the signs.

"Nothing happened after that for years. I never stopped thinking about it, though. Then one night, when I was fifteen, I couldn't sleep, and I got up from my bed. I looked out of the third-floor window, and I saw a person in the maze. I couldn't see his face, but I perceived it was a boy. I was sure it was one of my cousins. He waved to me, beckoned me to come. I ran downstairs as quietly as I could and stole outside. By then the figure was gone. I went all alone into the maze, overgrown as it was, and I was sure it was full of spirits as well. Then I went to the gazebo and waited and waited for the boy to come back. I stayed there all night. At last the sky lightened, and I saw I had been tricked. The spirit that had waved to me was not coming back, was not going to teach me the maze. I was still just a lowly housemaid with nothing before me but cleaning and laundry and caring for the Taylors' new daughter, Miss Harriet, Mr. Charles being so much older.

"But I promised myself then that I would bide my time, and when the power of the maze made itself known again, as it was bound to do, I would be ready for it.

"I suspected William." She looked down at Winnie.

"And was it him?" asked Winnie, afraid to hear yes, afraid to hear no.

"I asked him and he didn't deny it. I said I would tell Miss Harriet, and he said she'd never believe me. I told him I'd tell the villagers then, and he was wild for me not to. I said he must give me the secret. He escaped instead. Now you come, yet you say you don't know the maze! You got through it somehow. You'll try it again, and I'll be right behind you."

"I don't know about the maze, and I didn't understand Aunt Sally," said Winnie in a toneless voice.

"You'll understand the villagers if they come for you."

"What'll they do?"

"What they always do!"

"Nothing!" Alfred said, interrupting. "They'll not lay a hand on you."

"What could you do about it if they did?" said Violet.

They rode in silence the rest of the way to Crescent Ridge.

CHAPTER
THIRTEEN
CHAPTER
THIRTEEN
CHAPTER
THIRTEEN
CHAPTER
THIRTEEN
CHAPTER
THIRTEEN
CHAPTER
THIRTEEN
CHAPTER
THIRTEEN

Lily greeted Winnie with a smile that faded when she saw Winnie's face. "What's wrong?" she whispered as she helped Winnie hop in from the wagon.

"Everyone must stay in the house," Violet Minot commanded as she went through to the kitchen. "No one is to go outside!" She slammed the hallway door behind her.

Lily and Winnie stood and whispered in the front hall. "We saw Aunt Sally, but I couldn't make any sense out of what she said. She kept saying 'two' and holding up two fingers, and the last thing she said was 'Find the shadow.' There's nothing but shadows in the maze. She's too old, she can't talk very well. Mrs. Minot thinks I know how to get away, and she says she's going to follow me everywhere. And there were these awful people from the village! They kept crowding around like they wanted to get at me." Winnie imagined the villagers, coming in a bunch to Crescent Ridge. What if they came tomorrow? "I want to try again tonight. I saw Tab in the maze last night, too, and if she's there again, maybe I can follow her through."

"What if she isn't?"

"I don't know what I'll do. But if I wait, and Aunt Harriet comes back and tears up the woods, then I won't have any chance at all. Aunt Harriet is going to be kind of disappointed when she finds out about William."

"What about him? Did you find something out?"

"Mrs. Minot says he told her he's the maze-maker."

"What does that mean?"

"He's some kind of a witch or something. He's the cousin from so long ago—remember? He's probably gone for good to some other time. She wouldn't want to marry a witch anyhow, do you think?"

"William is two hundred years old? She'll never believe that. She'll think Violet is insane. But she surely will be sad if he doesn't come back."

"I guess what I'll do is wait till everybody has gone to bed, and then just try to get out of here as quietly as I can. If you hear Violet come after me,

☽

could you make some kind of commotion and make her think she has to run back to your room?"

Lily nodded. "One good thing is that she doesn't know how much better your foot is."

"It is?"

"Look. You've been standing on it ever since we came in."

Winnie looked down. It was true. "I'll keep acting like it hurts as much as ever."

Something creaked behind the closed hallway door. They heard rustling sounds and soft footsteps. A door opened and shut. "It's only Clara putting away linens," said Lily.

Supper was supposed to be punctually at six. At five-thirty Winnie sat in her room, trying to make herself stay calm. Lily had rebandaged her ankle, tying the strips of cloth as tightly as she could, and Winnie had practiced small, careful steps. Her toes were starting to look a little strange from the tight bandage, but she could get her foot into a sock and probably into her sneaker.

It seemed like bad luck to imagine the outcome beforehand, but she couldn't help herself. It was possible that tonight she would be sleeping in her own bed at home, and underneath her own chest of drawers she would once again find her beloved lost socks and dustballs. She could just imagine her homecoming—they might not even believe it was her. She checked herself in the mirror. She did look pretty much the same.

She reined her thoughts in and concentrated on how she would get down the front steps.

☀

Mrs. Minot yawned. "That trip to Aunt Sally's has worn me out," she said. They were eating boiled, unpeeled potatoes and boiled, unpeeled carrots and boiled cabbage and more pieces of leftover lamb, very small, hard pieces, doused in gray gravy. Winnie wouldn't have had much appetite, anyway. Clara had made two applesauce cakes, and their fragrance nearly canceled out the smell of the vegetables. But even the cake didn't make her hungry.

Mrs. Minot yawned again.

Winnie was expecting to be imprisoned in her room, but Mrs. Minot seemed to forget about that and instead declared that she was going to bed early. Alfred gave her an odd look.

"Come on, Alfred! I have things to discuss."

Clara collected the dishes to wash, and Lily and Winnie trailed away down the hall, Winnie saying "Ouch!" every few steps to keep up appearances. They closed the door to Winnie's room. Lily checked the bandage to make sure it was still tight, and Winnie eased her foot into her shoe.

"I'll be watching from my window," said Lily. "If you don't come back, I'll know you made it through. I just wish you could come back, if you figure out how to do it. I never had a friend like you."

"Me, either," said Winnie.

"Bye," whispered Lily, and she went away down the hall.

Winnie's heart began to pound. Though the

sky was still light, twilight colors were gathering across the green, and the shadows were longer. It was probably better to wait until it was dark, but finally she couldn't stand it any longer. She couldn't hear any noises in the house, so she opened her door. There sat Alfred, on the floor, in his stocking feet, leaning against the wall opposite. Winnie let out a little scream.

"Violet put me out here to make sure you stayed in your room," he said. "Now let's be a good girl and go back in. You mustn't disobey your elders, especially if they're subject to tantrums."

"I couldn't help it if I couldn't understand Aunt Sally."

"Violet's a determined woman."

"I just thought I'd look for something to read in the library."

"Never mind reading tonight. Back you go now."

Winnie went back in and shut the door. She stretched out on her bed and covered her face with her hands. Sooner or later Alfred would go to sleep, either in the hall or in his own bed, and she would try again. She turned her pillow over, and the calico mouse dropped to the floor. She had forgotten it was there. She picked it up and stuck it in her pocket.

It got dark slowly. Every now and then Winnie heard Alfred making noises in the hall, shifting his position, yawning, grumbling to himself. Then for a long time there was no sound at all. She slipped off the bed and opened her door a crack. Alfred's head was down on his chest, and he gave a kind of snort or snore that rattled his frame and then subsided. She took a couple of steps, watching. He was soundly asleep. Better not leave her door open. She reached back to close it, then limped along the corridor to the front stairs. At the turn by the landing she glanced back. He was still asleep. She went down the stairs, hanging on to the banister to keep weight off her foot, and at the bottom she looked up one more time. It was too dark to see if anyone was at the top of the staircase. She turned and hurried out the front door.

The stretch of grass before her seemed endless. Her legs moved like mechanical sticks, but the tight bandage kept her ankle from hurting. As she went past the barn someone whispered her name.

"Thomas?" she answered.

"Over here." She pulled the latch of the barn door from its slot, opened the door, slipped in, and pulled it to. "Where are you?" she said into the pitch-dark.

"I've got the cat," said Thomas. "Lily said you were going to try to follow her tonight, so I've been keeping her here with me." Winnie's eyes were slow getting used to the dark. Faint light and dark shapes began to organize themselves before her. Tab's white fur was almost phosphorescent. She brushed up against Winnie's legs.

Winnie turned to open the barn door. She could see Thomas now, in the semidarkness. When she was home again, he would no longer exist.

☽

"You have to go now." Thomas put his hand on her shoulder.

"I'm going. Thank you, thank you for the cat." She bent down and picked up Tab and held her firmly in both arms. Then she opened the door and stepped out. Tab immediately began to struggle free of Winnie's hold. She let out a loud meow. "Quiet!" Winnie snapped. The cat squirmed harder, gave an elastic leap, and slithered out of Winnie's arms. Winnie took a few hobbling steps after her, but she was nowhere near as fast. She reached into her pocket, pulled out the catnip mouse, and tossed it on the grass. She gave a quick glance toward the big house. Nothing stirred, though there might have been a pale shape in Lily's window. Tab leapt on the toy and batted it around. Winnie limped over and caught up with her. She shook one end of the mouse as Tab held it in her teeth. She reached forward to grab the cat, and Tab let go and ran off in the opposite direction, toward the house, leaping through the tall grass like a miniature tiger.

Winnie could have cried with exasperation. She tossed the mouse on the grass again and waited. A few moments later, out of the shadows sprang Tab, who took one long leap and captured the mouse. Winnie reached the maze fence, hobbled around to the gate, scrambled up, and slid down on the other side, landing with an off-balance jump on her good foot. She waited. She could see Tab's white silhouette in the black shrub-

❁

bery halfway up the hill, leaping and batting at the toy. "Here, puss," Winnie called. She hoped the sound wouldn't carry far. Tab turned and trotted straight for the maze. She eased under the gate, her back sliding into a *U*, and dropped the mouse at Winnie's feet. Winnie grabbed one end, and they tussled for it. Winnie yanked it away and tossed it several yards to the left. Tab leapt on it, shook it, and ran with it. The cat moved along a big curve, trotting so swiftly that it was hard to keep her in sight.

Winnie and the cat went all around the maze on one long circuit. The hedges were thick and prickly, but Winnie clawed them out of the way. Now she stumbled on a hedge trunk looping out of the dirt, now she snagged her foot in a root; at least she didn't fall. She could see the gate coming up again as she completed the circle. In front of her, Tab turned all the way around and started on a curve farther in. This was beginning to feel like something Winnie had done before. As she turned, dizzily following, she noticed she was stepping in a sunken place in the ground, and the curve Tab was following was all a little lower than the surrounding earth. No wonder she had turned her ankle the other night. She seemed to be running in a shallow ditch or trench—and then it came to her: these were the trenches from long ago, filled in with dirt and gravel, but sunken over the years.

At the end of the circle she and Tab went around one more time without changing direction,

☽

149

a still smaller circle. Then Tab dropped the mouse and began to tease it again. "Don't stop now," Winnie said with a moan. She had to reach down, shake the mouse by its skinny cloth tail, and tempt Tab into running once more. But as they passed the gate, by now barely visible through the bushes, Violet Minot climbed over. She saw Winnie. She said nothing but started off immediately, running parallel to Winnie. She must have been waiting for Alfred to tell her when to come out. So that was why Winnie had found it so easy to get by him.

Winnie went faster, panting noisily with the effort of pushing through the underbrush. It was possible that Violet had started off in the wrong direction, but if Winnie tried to figure that out, she'd get all mixed up. She felt the ground dip again.

She could hear Mrs. Minot crashing through the hedges. Neither of them spoke—there was only the noise of panting, the effort to break through the branches. Mrs. Minot came so close on this round that she almost touched Winnie. Her eyes, wide open, looked silver. She was taking no shortcuts; she knew the necessity of following the prescribed path.

Winnie looked down. She was getting closer to the center. Back one circle in the reverse direction. Ahead of her scampered Tab, but Winnie didn't need her anymore. She was being pulled along the curves of the maze. *Don't get dizzy*, she told herself. Mrs. Minot was getting closer. Two more circles,

❋

150

and there at last was the clearing, the sundial, and the scummy pond. A humming noise started to ring in her ears. She had forgotten about that: it meant the maze was working. Go straight for the middle—and out of nowhere she suddenly recalled Aunt Sally's forlorn figure, lost in her shabby chair, holding up two fingers. Did she mean to go around twice? Or that two people would go through? Find the shadow? Sundials made shadows. She went around the sundial once, twice, as Mrs. Minot's long, ivory hands reached out toward her. She was beside Winnie, and then Winnie and Mrs. Minot were pressed together into a squeezed, black void, an awful intimacy, with the housekeeper's dress rustling against Winnie's face and the deceivingly wholesome smell of apple cake on her apron; Mrs. Minot's hands reached for Winnie and tugged at her waist. Winnie bent forward against the flattening pressure, wrenched herself away from the grasping fingers, staggered two more steps—and then in rough gray pieces the rain-soaked asphalt and chain-link fence and clouded sky opened out all around her. She stumbled through alone. Harry was still standing there, and the couple with the dachshund were just turning out of sight.

CHAPTER FOURTEEN

When Winnie smelled the rain-drenched street—the wet asphalt and dripping leaves—and heard the squelching sound tires make on wet pavement, she knew for sure that she was back.

"Hey, what happened?" asked Harry. "Are you okay?"

A block away, on Center Street, a bus moaned and whined as it accelerated away from the curb. Horns blasted in a line of stalled traffic. A jackhammer tattered the air, and up toward the corner, under a yellow tarp, the crew of an electric-company truck hung around a manhole passing things down to someone at the bottom.

"Winnie! Say something! You disappeared, I swear!"

"I'm okay," said Winnie.

"What happened? Where were you?"

"You'll never believe it."

"What? Tell me!"

"I went back in time. This maze takes you to another century. I went back to 1889."

Harry pressed his lips together, and his ears, which already stuck out, seemed to reach a little farther from the sides of his head. "You went back a hundred years? The maze made you do that?"

"Yes. And there's someone back there that was following me. She might come through now, right now!"

Harry backed away from the painted lines. "The cat came through. Is that who you mean?"

"No. She did? Where did she go?"

"She's probably around here somewhere. She turned up a few minutes ago. I didn't see where from, and she came over and kind of meowed at my leg. So I gave her the catnip mouse. Then she ran all around the maze again, like before, and disappeared. She ran out again, just now, right before you did."

"Where's Daisy?"

"Over there." Harry pointed to the carriage. "Hey, you've only been gone ten minutes."

Winnie's stomach started to feel queasy. "Wait a minute. What day is it?"

"Tuesday."

153

"I think I was gone a lot longer than that. I want to go home." She limped over to the carriage.

"What'd you do to your foot?" The bandage was coming unwound, and the top of her misshapen ankle had swelled out over the edge of her sneaker. It was hurting worse now than it had at Crescent Ridge.

"I sprained my ankle back there."

"Want me to come home with you? You don't look too good. Jessica can wait."

She had forgotten about Jessica.

"Let's go," said Harry. "I'm getting soaked."

Winnie's mother was just closing the refrigerator door when Winnie came in, clutching Daisy. "Mom!" she burst out, and rushed over, hugging her mother clumsily around Daisy.

"What's got into you?" Her mother half laughed, scooping the baby out of Winnie's grasp. Winnie's heart was pounding, pounding, and for a minute she squeezed her mother with both arms and thought nothing could ever make her let go. Her mother was the same, the kitchen was the same—in fact, part of breakfast was still sitting there in the frying pan, uneaten, a pancake and a piece of cold bacon, left from a week ago. Two weeks? She wasn't sure how long she had been gone.

"Where's Lew?" Winnie asked.

"He just left for work. What's wrong? Did something happen?" She stepped away from Winnie and glanced down. "What have you done to your ankle?"

☀

154

"Twisted it."

"Let me see. Sit down. Here, Harry, your turn." She handed Daisy to Harry.

"Ouch!" Winnie yelled as her mother pulled off her sneaker.

"I'm going to call the doctor. This looks awful. What have you got tied around it? And look at you—you're covered with mosquito bites! Where have you been?"

Mrs. Baker called the health center, and Winnie heard her say she would bring Winnie over at twelve-thirty.

"Can Harry stay for a while?" Winnie begged.

"I don't mind. But you've got to stay off that foot. You have to keep it up. You remind her, Harry."

Harry telephoned Jessica and said he'd be home for lunch, and would she be sure to fix him three hot dogs, not just two? He and Winnie went into the den. Winnie propped her feet up on the coffee table, and Harry sprawled out on his stomach on the floor.

As soon as her mother was out of hearing range, Winnie told Harry everything about Crescent Ridge.

"It's a good thing you got out of there when you did," said Harry.

"I know it."

"I sort of wish I had gone."

"I wanted you to come. Why didn't you?"

"I never said I would, and it was freaky seeing you disappear."

☽

"What did I look like?"

"You went just the way the cat did, from the feet up. I was just making up my mind to go get somebody when you came back."

"Well, I made it, and I'll never have anything to do with that maze again!"

"But, Winnie," said Harry slowly, "the maze is still there."

"So what?" said Winnie after a minute.

"Somebody else could go in it."

"I don't want to think about that anymore." Winnie didn't even want to think about Lily or Thomas, as if that might conjure them up and she would find herself back in past time again. "Want to watch TV?" she asked.

"I could go in it, if I decided to," said Harry, ignoring her. "But I'm not going till I know all about getting back out."

"Believe me, it isn't so easy."

"It could be easy if you knew how ahead of time."

"I'm not sure I could ever do it again. Guess you could always take Tab."

"I've got a better idea. What about the person who painted the maze? Someone had to."

"William was the mazemaker, that's all I know." Winnie shrugged. Her mind was backing away from all of it.

"Then if it was him, he must have come here, to 1989, don't you see? He's probably still around here. Unless he went off to some other century."

"I wish you hadn't've thought of that," said Winnie.

"I want to try to find him."

The pediatrician took one look at Winnie's ankle and said, "When did this happen?"

"Just this morning," said Mrs. Baker.

"Oh, it's an older injury than that," said the doctor, giving Mrs. Baker a suspicious glance. He had Winnie's ankle X-rayed to be on the safe side, and then he wound an elastic bandage around it.

"That really feels a lot better," said Winnie.

"I should think so. Next time come in promptly. We can save you a lot of discomfort."

"That's not our regular doctor," said Mrs. Baker on the way home. "Your ankle was perfectly all right this morning, no matter what he said."

"I know." Winnie nodded. "It just turned purple awfully fast."

"Oh, well. Doctors have to be extra careful these days, or they get sued. I'm so relieved it's only a sprain."

Winnie slept on the couch all afternoon and woke up only when Lew came home and set his briefcase down with a thump.

"You're home!" she exclaimed, and hopped on one foot down the hall, beaming at him, and grabbed him around the waist in a giant hug.

"Was there any doubt?" Lew joked. "It's always nice to get a hearty welcome. Hey—you've hurt yourself. What happened?"

☽

*   *   *

Winnie was excused from table-setting chores, but she sat in the kitchen for the company, her foot propped up, chattering and snapping the ends off string beans and listening to Daisy squawk. She kept leaving her sentences unfinished, though, and she couldn't keep her mind on what anyone was saying.

She decided she was tired, that was all, and she could hardly wait to go to bed. She crawled beneath the sheets, in her own bed at last, and closed her eyes, hoping she would fall asleep instantly. Instead she thrashed around and kept turning her pillow over to the cool side. Just when she thought she was finally sleepy, another cord of anxiety would jerk her awake.

She realized later that she must have fallen asleep, but her dream was so vivid, she could have been wide-awake. She was strolling by the nursing home, just to have a look at it and see what she could recognize from the old house. When she got to the fence and peeked through the slats, the nursing home wasn't there. A brick apartment building, three stories high, occupied most of the land. There was a gravel parking lot filled with cars, and some small new trees, their skinny trunks wrapped in white strips, dotted the remaining grass. When she looked a little closer, she saw that the apartment building was insubstantial, like a mirage or a drawing on tracing paper. Behind the filmy bricks, the sturdy clapboards of the nursing home showed through.

She stopped a man in the street and asked what had happened to the nursing home, and the man said there wasn't one and never had been. So she pointed and asked if the building didn't look flimsy, and he said no, it looked fine; as a matter of fact, he lived there. He walked across the parking lot and went into the building. A moment later Winnie saw him appear in a second-story window, and then someone snapped down the shade—someone with a thin arm in a long black sleeve.

Winnie's eyes flew open, and she sat up. For a moment she couldn't remember which was actually there, the nursing home or the apartment building, and her memory of Crescent Ridge was blotted out, too. Then she sorted out actuality—the nursing home—and she could remember Crescent Ridge again. But the feeling of the dream wouldn't leave her. Could Mrs. Minot have already maneuvered her way into the distant past and changed things? Winnie had no way of knowing what had happened to Violet Minot. If she succeeded, there was no end to what the consequences would be.

"I'm *not* going back in!" she shouted. The sound of her own voice startled her and rang through the sleeping household as well. In a minute Winnie heard a door on the first floor click open and shut, and Lew came treading up the back stairs barefoot, tying his bathrobe sash.

"What's the trouble here?" he asked, peering

☾

159

sleepily at Winnie. "Are you having a bad dream?" He ran his hand through his hair, which made it stand straight up, and sat down on the edge of Winnie's bed.

Winnie huddled next to him. "I dreamed that someone had gone backward in time and was changing the past, and everything was starting to be different. If that was real, what would happen?"

"If what was real?"

"Changing things that have already happened. If you could, would everything after that be different?"

"You can't, but if you could—let me see, if you changed one thing, then probably what came after that would be slightly changed, too. And what came after that would be changed a little more, and so on. This is a puzzle to talk about in the morning."

She flopped back down on her stomach and let Lew tuck the sheet around her shoulders. "Now go to sleep, and no more bad dreams," he said. "If a nightmare starts up, you tell it to stop, right in your dream."

The stairs creaked as Lew went down them. In the distance Winnie heard him open and close the bedroom door. She must have slept soundly then. When she did get up in the morning, she felt fine, her ankle didn't hurt much, and she knew she had to get down to Harry's, no matter what.

"Can I go down to the Austins'?" she asked as she was finishing breakfast. She had had two huge glasses of orange juice. "Please? I'll baby-sit later on." Her mother nodded yes. She ran, tender ankle and all, to Harry's house and banged on the front door. Jessica answered.

"Where's Harry? Quick!"

"Gosh, slow down!" said Jessica as Winnie shoved past her.

Harry was slouched over the breakfast table spooning cereal into his mouth. Slouching over significantly shortened the distance from the dish to his lips.

"Harry—we do have to find William! I just realized—I had a bad dream—if Violet Minot gets the maze and uses it to change things, there's no telling what'll happen. We've got to warn William. Maybe he can undo it somehow."

"What?" said Harry. Winnie had been talking very fast, and he simply watched her the way he might look at the Tilt-a-Whirl at the fairgrounds. He turned back to his cereal. He shook some broken pieces into his dish, upended the box, and slapped it a couple of times. He groaned and peeked into the paper lining. "Gone," he said. He spooned up the few shreds that floated in the leftover milk.

"And that's not all. I think William *was* around here not long ago, because remember when you asked me on the phone if I'd seen Tab, the same morning I went into the maze? And I said I thought she had an owner, after all? That must have been him I saw, in my driveway." Winnie was out of breath.

☽

Harry stared at her.

"Is this something you saw on TV?" asked Jessica.

"No, at the schoolyard," said Harry.

Jessica began to unload the dishwasher.

"Jessica," said Harry, "you don't happen to know the guys who spray-paint the school and all, do you?"

"Not me. I don't hang around with them."

"Do you know anybody who does?"

"I might. How come?"

"There's a maze over at the Morrissey School, painted on the asphalt, and it has this weird power. It takes you to another time if you walk through it right."

"What do you mean, another time? Mountain standard?"

"Another century," said Winnie. "I went in it and traveled back a hundred years."

Jessica put her hands on her hips and cocked her head.

"It sounds crazy, I know," said Winnie. "But it did happen. Harry saw me disappear."

"Jessica," said Harry, "forget the time-travel part and just tell us about the spray-painters."

"My sister hangs out with some kids that might know."

"Can you ask her?" said Winnie. "Right now? Is she at home? Can you call her?"

"Wait a second! She's at work. She's down at Rix Discount."

☀

"Don't they have a phone?"

Jessica sighed. "Okay."

Winnie and Harry stood at Jessica's elbow while she made the call. "I still want to try it myself," muttered Harry. Winnie guessed from overhearing half the conversation that Jessica's sister did know something.

"What is it? What did she say?" Winnie could hardly stand to wait for Jessica to shove her gum into her cheek and tell them.

"Judy says she knows what you're talking about. She says nobody's been back there since this fellow painted it, because he got into trouble with the cops, and now there's police there every night."

"Who was he?"

"They didn't know him. He was hanging around the schoolyard. That's where lots of Judy's friends hang out, but she herself doesn't, so don't get the wrong idea. My parents'll kill her if they find out.

"This guy they never saw before is hanging around there acting strange. He kept walking around in circles. Then he'd leave, then he'd come back and walk around some more. He never said anything to them. He was real short, and looked like he was dressed for a part in some movie.

"One night one of Judy's friends brought a can of spray paint, just to do a little bit, and this same man came out of the bushes and asked if he could have it when this fellow was done with it. The guy said sure. He gave it to him, and then they saw him

☽

163

start spraying this big circle, and littler circles inside, just that very design you were talking about. A maze. When he was halfway done, a police car came along. My sister's friends ran away, but this guy didn't even notice. He's concentrating so hard, he only looks up when the car stops, puts on its blue light and headlights, and the door opens."

"How does your sister know all this?"

"Well, her friends ran away, but not far. They wanted to see what would happen."

"So then what?" Winnie asked.

"The cop gets out and walks over. The guy doing the spray-painting goes a little faster, then stands back to see what he's done, and goes at it again. The cop, instead of jumping on him at first, stands back and puts his arms over his chest, like, 'You gotta be kidding me, buddy, is this for real?' Watching him. Then the man is finished. His design or maze, whatever, is done. He walks over, then hands the can of paint to the cop! The cop says, 'Gee, thanks,' in this incredibly sarcastic voice. The man starts to walk away. The cop leaps out and grabs him by the back of his arm and starts to yell at him. The guy is completely confused. He tries to run, can't get anywhere. The last they see of him, he's got handcuffs on, and into the back of the car he goes."

"Did they take him to jail?" asked Harry.

"You'd have to go to the police station to find that out. I kind of doubt if they'd put you in prison for spray-painting."

✺

"Do you think he's still there now?" asked Winnie.

"This all happened a few days ago, so I don't guess he would be. They said he talked with a funny accent. Maybe he was foreign and didn't understand about policemen, I don't know."

"What was his name?" asked Winnie.

"Nobody knows him. They don't know his name or where he comes from."

"It must be him," said Winnie.

"Must be," said Harry. "Jessica, can you call the jail?"

"No! I most certainly can*not!*"

"But it's important."

"They won't tell you stuff like that over the phone, and I'm not going to call them even if they will. If you want to know who's in jail, you had better go yourselves."

"Okay," said Harry.

Jessica gave him a disgusted look. "This is something you have to check with your mom about. No, Harry, you cannot go visit the jail, so don't try to talk me into it."

Harry threw a wet sponge at Jessica.

CHAPTER FIFTEEN

Mrs. Baker was waiting in the kitchen for Winnie. "I'm going to the grocery store," she said. "I won't be more than an hour, and Daisy's asleep."

"Okay."

Winnie stood on the back steps and watched the old station wagon back down the driveway. Then she darted out and waved her arms. "Mom! Wait! Before you go, can I ask you something?"

Her mother braked the car. "What is it?"

"If you wanted to find someone and you didn't have any idea where they were, how could you do it?"

"The police, I suppose. They have a missing-persons department."

"But besides the police, what would you do?"

"Goodness! Put an ad in the classified section of the newspaper?"

"But what would you do if you were a kid and not a grown-up?"

"Winnie, who is missing? What are you talking about?"

"Harry and I are playing sort of a game."

"Well, I'll think about it while I'm at the store. See you later."

Winnie hunted through the newspaper for the section marked CLASSIFIED. There weren't any categories for MISSING or PERSONS, though there were three under PERSONALS, for people who wanted a date. It didn't seem likely that William would read a newspaper, anyway, and the ads cost twenty-six dollars besides.

They could put up signs around their neighborhood, the way people did to find lost pets. Winnie found a marker and sketched out a poster on a blank piece of typing paper: WANTED! MAZE-MAKER! CALL WINNIE AT 555-8330. She could ask Lew to Xerox it at his office, and she and Harry could tape them to lampposts. In the meantime they could search for him themselves.

In the early afternoon Harry and Winnie met at Winnie's driveway with their bikes and went off to ride around the pond. The broad asphalt path was crowded with joggers and people walking dogs. They didn't really expect to find William in a pair of jogging shorts and running shoes. They locked their bikes to a park bench and climbed past the

☽

gray tree stump to the top of the hill, looking in the bushes and grass for anybody who might be trying to hide. They stopped short when Harry spotted a blanket on the ground next to a tree, and they could see that there was a shape, a person, under the blanket. A rusty shopping cart, piled high with lumpy plastic bags, stood right beside the blanket. As Winnie looked closer, the blanket stirred, a head turned over, and a sleeping face showed itself. The face was that of a man around Lew's age, grimy, deeply tanned, with dark hair falling across his face in greasy strings. His mouth was half open, and beneath his head Winnie could see the bunched-up rag he was using for a pillow.

She and Harry turned quietly away and scrambled back downhill to their bikes. "That can't be him," said Harry.

They rode slowly around one more time, then crossed the parkway at Liff Circle and pushed their bikes up the sidewalk toward Winnie's house.

"What else can we do?" Winnie said. "We could walk around here for days and never find a trace of him. If Tab was here, I'd figure William was still here, too, but she hasn't been around to my house. I haven't heard any cats meowing anywhere."

"Want to take one more look at the schoolyard?" asked Harry.

"Might as well."

They rode on the sidewalk, wobbling because they were going slowly. Winnie looked through the stockade fence half fearfully, afraid she would blink and find a strange building on the other side. But everything looked as it always did—the house with its awnings, the metal chairs, a few old people sitting in the sun talking. At the top of the slope to the schoolyard, though, Harry stopped and said, "Uh-oh."

Winnie pulled up beside him, balancing on her bike seat with her toes just touching the ground. She looked down. The maze had faded. She could still see its outlines, but the silver was faint and it no longer glowed.

"Do you suppose he's gone?" she said.

"I don't know."

"What if he's dead?"

"If he's dead, we've had it."

"He wouldn't let himself get killed."

"He wouldn't have to, as long as he stayed close to his maze. He could always escape."

"I'm not giving up." The stretch of rough asphalt looked worn-out, deserted even by stray dogs. The only living thing Winnie could see was an ugly bunch of crabgrass poking up through a crack. Though the day was hot, there was a chill in the air that blew over them.

"What would happen if we drew the maze again?" said Winnie.

Harry began to nod slowly.

"He might come to it, don't you think? No matter where he is, he'd know if someone was trying to bring back the maze."

"Maybe. We can't use spray paint, though," said Harry. "We'd get caught for sure."

☽

"It probably doesn't matter what we use, because the real maze is still there, way underneath the asphalt. We'll go over the whole thing to make it show up. We could use plain old chalk."

"We better do it soon."

"I know. How about right now?"

"What if somebody walked by and saw us?"

"Okay. We'll do it tonight."

Harry heaved a sigh.

"Are you afraid?"

"It's not that. But how can we get out after dark? Your mom will *never* let you go. It's not so easy to sneak out, either. My mom wakes up for everything."

"I'm not afraid to, either."

They were both quiet for a moment, thinking of how unafraid they were. Then Harry gave his bike pedals a tremendous backward spin. "I've got it. My dad has this tent that we use when we go camping in Montana. Let's ask if we can put it up outside in the backyard and sleep in it. Then, when it's late enough and nobody's looking, we can come over here."

"Okay!"

"I'll ask him when he gets home tonight. He's going to say yes, I know it. He loves to put that tent up."

"Call me as soon as you find out."

They rode off separately.

*   *   *

At six o'clock, as the evening news came on, Winnie set the table for supper without being asked. "Is there anything else you'd like me to do?" she asked her mother sweetly. Her mother gave her a wry smile. "Sure. You can wash some lettuce, and you can tell me what you want. I can tell there's something."

Winnie fished in the refrigerator vegetable drawer and found a head of odd-looking lettuce among some carrots that were so old, they had sprouted white hair-roots. She filled the sink with cold water and began to swish the lettuce leaves around. "Well, Harry and I want to sleep outside in a tent in back of his house tonight. If his dad says it's okay."

"Is that all?"

"You mean, it's all right?"

"I think so. The Austins are careful, and their yard is fenced."

The phone rang as Winnie was twirling the salad spinner. "I'll get it!" She leapt for the receiver. "Hello? Harry?"

"Yep, it's me. My dad says okay." A tingle of fear started up Winnie's back. "Come over around seven-thirty, and bring your sleeping bag."

After supper Winnie crammed her sleeping bag into its sack and put on a pair of jeans and a turtleneck. She looked through her shelves and found a box with several broken pieces of white chalk. She put that in her school backpack and stuck in her flashlight as well.

☽

171

"See you in the morning," she said to Lew and her mother. They were still at the table, finishing bowls of peaches and taking turns jiggling Daisy on their shoulders.

"Want me to walk up with you?" asked Lew.

"Sure."

Harry's dad had already driven the stakes into the ground, and Harry was holding up the center of the tent while his father fixed the frame. Mr. Austin was much quieter and smaller than Mrs. Austin. He wore glasses and had a handlebar mustache. "We'll be done in a few minutes," he called to them. He pushed the last aluminum tube into place, and the tent stood alone. "Now," he said, "I'll sleep out on the back porch here, while you're in the tent, and then you'll feel perfectly safe."

"No!" exclaimed Winnie and Harry at the same time.

"Dad! That'll ruin it!"

"Your mother thought it was a good idea. What if you wake up in the middle of the night and get scared?"

"We'll be okay. We don't need a grown-up!"

"Well, what if your mother and I wake up and we get scared?"

"Then sleep with all your bedroom windows open. We'll be fine. Honest," said Harry.

"I'll leave this battle to you, Garrett," said Lew with a laugh. "Good night, all." He kissed Winnie on the forehead and left.

Mr. Austin finally agreed to sleep inside, with the windows open, and Winnie and Harry crawled into the tent. They spread out their sleeping bags and waited for dark.

"It stays light the longest of all in June," said Harry.

"We've got to wait till it's very late, anyhow," said Winnie. "At least midnight." She rolled over on her back and clicked her flashlight on and off, shining it on the tent ceiling. "Did you bring anything to eat?"

"Yes." Harry pulled a bag of cheese popcorn from the corner of the tent. Winnie ate a few pieces, but her mouth was dry and she could hardly swallow.

"Are you worried about finding him?" asked Harry.

"I'm worried about what he'll be like," said Winnie. "What if he can't understand us? What if he traps us into going with him?"

"That's a crazy idea."

"It's not. He could do anything."

They stayed awake for a long time. Harry had brought out his Monopoly set, but neither of them could get interested enough to keep playing. At some point, without meaning to, they fell asleep.

Winnie woke up suddenly and shook Harry. "What time is it? Wake up!"

"I don't know. I didn't bring the alarm clock."

"I think we slept too long!" Winnie crawled to

☽

173

the tent flap and looked out. Every house visible over the top of the fence was dark. No traffic noise came from Center Street. No cars went by in front of Harry's house. "Come on!" Winnie whispered. "It must be the middle of the night!"

Harry groaned and pushed back his sleeping bag. Winnie felt around frantically for the box of chalk. With shaking fingers she pushed it into her jeans' pocket. They crawled cautiously out of the tent and crept around the house on the side away from the open bedroom windows. They walked silently on the grass beside Harry's driveway and out into the middle of the street. The sky was black beyond the street lamps, and they moved without a sound from one pool of cold fluorescent light to the next. When they turned the corner of Lesser Road and were out of sight of Harry's house, Winnie realized she'd been holding her breath the entire time.

Every house on this street was dark, too, except for an occasional porch light. The bushes in the front yards seemed to have taken on personality in the dark, as if they had moved forward into a night life while the houses receded into sleep. Winnie couldn't make herself look at the nursing home. Then they reached the top of the asphalt slope and were walking down it. There was no moon, but purplish lights shone on the schoolyard. Winnie had forgotten it was lit.

"This is as bad as broad daylight," she whispered.

"Let's do it quick," said Harry.

The faded paint showed a little more brightly under the street lamps. Winnie took out a piece of chalk and handed it to Harry. She took another and began to rub it over the paint, starting in the center of the maze. "Don't start on the outside," she warned. It took several minutes, and the chalk wore out fast. Harry went around in one direction, Winnie in the other. Winnie left little crumbs behind as she worked, drawing faster now, making thinner lines, connecting them all. Her face got hot from bending over. At last they finished the outermost circles and brushed the chalk dust from their hands. "Let's wait over in that corner," she said.

They sat on the ground by the cyclone fence. Insects buzzed in the weeds behind them, and a distant truck shifted gears as it rumbled up Center Street on some lonely errand. The maze looked wavering and uncertain on the abandoned blacktop. They waited without talking.

A soft rustle behind them made Winnie jump. A few feet away, a plump raccoon scurried out of shelter, ambled across the corner of the schoolyard, and disappeared into the shrubbery on the far side.

They waited longer.

"He's got to come," Winnie whispered.

It seemed as though a couple of hours must have passed. Harry's head nodded every once in a while, and Winnie felt her eyes closing by themselves. She thought she saw a faint band of light in the sky over by Center Street, toward the east.

☽

When she next looked up, a man had stepped out of the shadow of the school. He wore a white shirt and a loose vest and a pair of pants that looked like knickers. Winnie went cold all over. He glanced in their direction, seemed not to see them, and walked back and forth with his back to them, staring at the maze. He was short—only a little taller than Winnie—and moved with an easy quickness, like the boys at school who were really good at sports.

Winnie scrambled to her feet. The man whipped around at the noise, saw them, and froze. "Who's there?" he called.

"Don't worry. We're only children."

"Why are you hiding there?"

"We've been trying to find you."

"I don't want to be found. Get back." He started to run around the first ring of the maze.

"Wait!" Winnie darted forward onto the chalked lines.

"Get back, or you could be caught!" He sounded angry. She backed away, and he started to run again.

"Please!" said Winnie. "I've got something to tell you from Aunt Harriet."

At that he stopped.

"I know her, because I went through your maze. That's why we have to talk to you."

"Who are you?"

"I'm Winnie Brown and this is Harry Austin."

"So it was you." He turned to face them. His eyes were wary, and he held himself tense, as if ready to run.

Blocks away, a police siren sounded. "Let's hide under the tree," said Harry. He and Winnie crouched down and crawled beneath the shadow of the dead oak. William sat down on the ground, well out of their reach.

"Don't try to stop me from going," he said. "I'll never spend another night in your prison."

"Did they put you in jail?" asked Harry.

"Yes." He stopped abruptly. Up close, he looked younger than he had when Winnie had first seen him—like someone just out of college. Winnie took in his curly hair and broken fingernails, the leather of his weskit, his coarse cloth knickers. His shoes were the oddest of all—somewhat triangular in shape, with a fastener on the side and soles as thick as boards. Winnie felt a momentary urge to capture him—he was small enough for Harry and her to overpower—and keep him long enough to satisfy herself that she had soaked up everything she could about him and his real time.

"Well," said Winnie, "what I wanted to say was, I went in your maze—by accident, really. I wasn't trying to take it over or anything, I just got fascinated by the cat, and I went back in time to Crescent Ridge. The people there are looking for you and really want you to come back. But it would be dangerous, because this woman Violet wants to get the maze, and she's murderously mad."

"She's no threat now," said William.

"She isn't?"

"No. She's caught. Only one person can go through the maze at a time, and if someone else is there with them, the second one can be trapped between years. When you came back, she was seized. She's frozen in time—in no one's time—forever.''

Winnie drew in her breath as she pictured Mrs. Minot, grasping hands outreached, stuck in midair.

"She'd have set the villagers on me," William went on. "That's why I left Harriet in the first place—they'd have killed me if they believed I was a witch. In my time that was common."

"But you aren't one," said Winnie cautiously.

He shook his head. "My grandmother was, though she never offended anyone. She gave me one of her tricks, but I'm nothing out of the ordinary."

"Can you teach the trick to someone else?" asked Harry.

"I promised I wouldn't."

"Are you going back?" Winnie asked.

"Back where? Perhaps to my grandmother—though there's nothing there for me, no land, no fortune. Not to my uncle's—my cousins would kill me. Not to Crescent Ridge—I've lost my chance there. But I won't stay in this time, either. I hate it here."

"You hate it?" said Winnie.

"I belong working the land, and there isn't any here. There's too much noise, besides."

"You should go back to Aunt Harriet," Winnie whispered.

He shook his head and looked away with the

same sad expression as had come over Aunt Harriet's face that first evening at Crescent Ridge, when Winnie and Lily had left her in the library.

"What was it like when you first learned about the maze?" asked Harry. "Are you sure you can't teach part of the trick to someone else?"

The faint light in the east had begun to spread by now, and William glanced over his shoulder at the sky.

"There's time to tell," said Harry. "The police won't come."

"Do you swear it?"

"We swear," said Winnie and Harry together.

William began to tell his story.

☽

CHAPTER SIXTEEN

"I first dug the maze because I was afraid of my cousins. This was in 1668. I had just come to the Colonies to live with my uncle, Richard Sparrow, and his family. They had come over from England seven years before, and the farming was hard. He had two sons, Fred and Seth, and they made fun of my curly hair and red cheeks. 'Should have been a girl, shouldn't you!' they would say. They were big and stiff, like blocks of wood, and clumsy and stupid. My uncle was mean with them, but he took to me right away. I worked hard and I was lucky. My ax head never broke. I never got sick. Pretty soon my uncle declared that I reminded him more of himself than his own sons did, and he intended to reward me for it. When he told me that, I had a feeling trouble would come of it.

"The second spring I was there, I finished digging the maze. It was a mizmaze, as we called it at home, and everyone ran races and games through it on May Eve. Everyone in my old village knew its shape, but before I left home, my grandmother had told me about the extra turn. It wasn't in our village maze, and she said she had intended never to tell me about it, so that the secret would die with her. But she couldn't help wanting to do for her own, especially as I had no other family. And perhaps she was not the only one who still knew; if that was so, she said, it was better that someone of her family have the secret as well.

"I listened, not quite believing her, but I did as I was told and learned where the extra turn should go and how to use it. I hated the moment when I had to leave. She pressed a loaf of bread and a piece of cheese into my satchel and hugged me tightly and told me all would be well. She gave me a kitten, one of her old cat's last litter, to tuck in my shirt and keep me company. Then she laughed and asked if she had to boot me out to get me on the road. I tried to laugh at that, and she hugged me, and then I practically ran, for to tell the truth, we were both crying.

"Now, in this second spring at my uncle's I had the notion to hold a May Eve celebration like the ones at home. It wasn't easy to persuade the

181

people round about, for they were a sober lot, but the preacher himself finally agreed. On that evening I stood in the road, waiting for the children. The maze lay behind me in a far corner of the field. They came along, some walking, some riding in clusters on horseback. They were all ages, a ragamuffin crew if you judged by their clothes; but some wore something special added by their mothers—a bit of lace or a ribbon. Most of them were barefoot. Their parents came, too.

"At first the children were shy and refused to join hands. I had to go around fastening them together. Then I led the line into the maze, around and around, until I got to the center—avoiding the extra turn, naturally. At the center I turned and wound all the way out, going past some children who were still coming in. Someone laughed, another lost his grip, and soon everyone was out of step and laughing and shouting to begin again. So they lined up once more, and the double spiral moved in and out of the maze. Even my cousins found places in the line, though the games were supposed to be only for the children.

"After this had gone on for some time, I brought out the cider. I had made it myself, from old winter apples. Everyone was thirsty, and they gulped it down, sharing cups or drinking from the jug.

"As soon as I tasted it, I knew something was wrong. Either it had started to spoil, or someone had put something in it. I took only one sip, but I saw Fred and Seth guzzle it down and urge everyone to have more. I tried to warn them, but no one listened to me.

"In no time the children became wild and silly, and the older ones got out of control, and then it turned into a mad scene, with people howling and running about, and pairs of the older ones stealing away as it got darker, and later being discovered asleep together behind a barn. The little ones got sick and were taken home by their parents, who had no kind words for me, nor for my uncle.

"Then it was only the three of us, me and Seth and Fred, standing by the maze in a flood of moonlight. Seth tossed a damp woolen sack onto the ground. A whining sound came out of it. I snatched it up, untwisted the top, and reached in. My hand closed around my cat, soaking wet, shivering. I dropped her inside my shirt to warm her. I could feel her icy claws scratching at my stomach.

" 'You run the maze,' said Seth to me, lurching on his drunken feet. I backed away, and Fred shoved me down. I got up on my feet. Fred hit me again, this time in the head, and I understood then that they would kill me with their bare hands if they could.

" 'The maze! You run it!' they shouted at me.

"I knew I could run faster than they could. They were stumbling behind, because they were drunk. I knew every inch of the ground from the hours I'd spent digging the paths, but the moon cast strange shadows. My foot caught on a root. I pushed myself back on balance with my hand. I wished I had left the paths even rougher. Fred and Seth kept falling, but they were strong and I knew they would catch up. They hooted and howled and cut across the trenches, coming straight for me. So I held the cat tightly to my chest—at least she would go with me—and I ran the extra turn."

"Did you know what would happen to you?" asked Winnie.

"Only that I would land many years in the future. When I got to Crescent Ridge, the maze was hidden by woods, and I thought I could safely leave it. Then I learned that the maze had been discovered when Violet Minot was a child, and that she not only remembered it, but also that she had been waiting all this time for a chance to try its powers. I hadn't thought of what would happen in all the years between, or that the maze would keep its force, and always would, until I closed it off."

"Are you going to?" asked Harry.

"I will never close it off."

"You mean, you'll just keep going from one time to another? And never stay anywhere?"

"If that's what I must do to stay alive."

"What if other people fall into the maze like me but don't end up getting out?" said Winnie. "Like the two boys who disappeared when Mrs. Minot was a girl. What happened to them?"

"They went through one after the other, but separately, so they weren't trapped. They landed in a time that was future to them, though past to you."

"But can't they go back?"

"Perhaps. I could find them and bring them back, though not exactly to the time when they left. They're older now. They will have to invent a story to explain their absence."

"So you will find them?"

William nodded.

"Their parents are going to be awfully glad, no matter how much older they are! And then will you go back to Crescent Ridge? You can stay there. What good does it do if you don't belong anywhere?"

William shook his head.

"You ought to go back, because Aunt Harriet is looking for you, and she said she would never stop."

"She did?"

"Yes." Winnie nodded emphatically. "She said *never*. She's rich, you know. She'll spend her whole life doing that, probably going all over the world, and it'll be hopeless, all because you're too stubborn or afraid to go back. So you'll make her waste her life."

William looked at her with puzzled eyes, as if unsure whether to believe her.

Light had spread halfway across the sky by now, and colors appeared above the brick walls of the school: pink and gold and blue. A fair day for sure, Winnie thought.

☽

William got to his feet.

"Are you going?" Winnie cried.

"Yes. I've told you everything you need to know, and you have done the same for me." He moved away from them.

"Good-bye, then." Winnie waved, and William gave a sort of salute. "Thank you," she thought she heard him say.

He ran the maze quickly, without even looking down to make sure of his way. As he got near the center a growling meow burst from the bushes, and Tab shot across the asphalt toward the maze. She scampered through the circles as William stood and waited for her. He reached down and scooped her up under his arm, and the two of them vanished together.

CHAPTER SEVENTEEN

That fall, the cold weather came early. By the end of October, kids were wearing their winter parkas every day, and it had even snowed one afternoon— gray, icy bits that whirled around in a blustery wind. But on Halloween the weather was warm. Winnie sat by her open front window, watching for trick-or-treaters and adjusting her cutlass. At five-thirty Mrs. Austin was going to pick her up and take both Winnie and Harry to a Halloween party. Winnie felt a pang of nostalgia as she saw the first sheet-draped ghost and dime-store Snow White and walking calculator come up the street, followed by a father who had painted his face to look like a

187

clown. She and Harry were too old to trick-or-treat. Daisy, on the other hand, was too young. Her mother had made Daisy a pumpkin costume, anyway, with orange tights and a green stem-hat.

Winnie was dressed as a pirate. She had a satin blouse with billowy sleeves that her mother had saved from the seventies, and she and her mother had made a black felt vest and had ripped the pants legs of an old pair of jeans so they looked ragged. She had even borrowed a sword from Mr. Martin up the street, who told her he had used it for dress parades in the Navy, but he hadn't had much call for it since. Her eye patch was held on by an elastic cord that bunched up her hair, so she decided to leave it off until they walked into the party.

"Still waiting?" asked her mother. She emptied another bag of miniature candy bars into the goodies bowl beside the front door. "It's so nice of Elaine to do this. If you keep doing things together, you and Harry will always stay friends."

"Right," said Winnie automatically. As far as she could tell, there was no reason why they wouldn't stay friends, whether parents took them to parties or not. At least the Austins hadn't moved, not this year, anyway.

"There she is!" Winnie jumped up, and her mother opened the door for her. Her mother waved to Mrs. Austin as Winnie got into the back seat. Winnie laid the sword on the floor by her feet and fastened her seat belt. "You look great!" she said to Harry. "What are you?" Harry was wearing his regular clothes. He picked up a dark rubber wad from the seat beside him and pulled it over his head. "A werewolf," Winnie said.

"You got it." Harry's voice sounded muffled.

Mrs. Austin drove them down the block and around the corner onto Lesser Road. She was driving slowly, in case someone from a group of children got excited and darted into the street. Winnie hadn't come this way for many weeks now. They passed the stockade fence, and then the schoolyard, the cyclone-fence gate still half off its hinges. The graffiti on the school walls looked garish in the dark—there was Casper, still floating across the windowless west doors, with his cartoon grin and round, white eyes.

Casper wasn't what Winnie was looking for. "There's nothing left of it now," she said to Harry. Harry leaned across to see out of Winnie's window.

For the rest of that summer they had gone back to the schoolyard every day, and day by day, beneath their chalk marks, the maze had faded. Winnie had sometimes stood there, thinking she heard a voice in the wind or saw a flash of white fur that could have been a cat. But nothing ever came, and the maze grew lighter and lighter, until all that was left were patches of lifeless gray paint. They hadn't wanted to draw over it again. They knew the power of the maze was gone; even so, they decided not to try it out. Winnie often wondered whether William had gone back to Aunt Harriet or had traveled to some other time; and she thought

☽

about Violet Minot, trapped between centuries—a hundred years now! Would she stay preserved as she was and one day pop out again? It didn't seem likely that Winnie would ever find out.

School had started after Labor Day. Up till then, the schoolyard had seemed like Winnie's territory, but now it belonged to the school again. Yellow buses waited in line and blocked the street; the blacktop was covered with mobs of kids; a janitor came out and asked what she and Harry were doing there. Winnie's school started a few days later. She was getting near to being one of the oldest students, and she liked that. She and Harry stopped going to the schoolyard, and Winnie didn't miss it.

The maze was gone, but tonight the air, so unexpectedly warm, felt and even smelled like summer. As they drove past and turned onto Center Street, Winnie suddenly could not get her mind off Crescent Ridge; it was as if the people had been there all along, waiting, and now they crowded into a cleared space in her mind. She heard Lily's voice and saw Thomas rowing them across the pond; she felt Aunt Harriet's cool, immaculate hand on her forehead, and she sat and shivered as Mrs. Minot whispered about keeping magic things to themselves. She hardly heard a word Harry or Mrs. Austin said to her as they drove the rest of the way to the party. Mrs. Austin parked the car, and as the three of them climbed the steps to the Hamilton Community Hall, Winnie turned to Mrs. Austin and said, "Is there any way to find out about people who lived a hundred years ago, but didn't get to be famous, like a president? I mean, can you find out what happened to them afterward?"

"After what?" asked Mrs. Austin. She opened the door and ushered them into a noisy swarm of goblins, rock stars, clowns, bears, princesses, Gypsies.

"In the rest of their lives."

"Well, sure. There are records of people's lives—letters, diaries, newspapers. Now, why aren't you dressed up?" Mrs. Austin asked a pair of girls standing by the door.

"We're fifties teenagers! Can't you tell?"

"Oh!" said Mrs. Austin, starting to laugh. "I didn't realize you were wearing costumes."

"Mom, how can you be so—?" Harry complained. He vanished into the crowd, and Winnie followed him.

Halloween was on a Thursday, and by Saturday morning it was freezing cold again, the sky gray and heavy with clouds. The air had a bite to it that signaled snow.

Winnie wandered up to Harry's house after lunch, actually hoping Mrs. Austin would be there, even if Harry wasn't. She was. Harry was at the hardware store, doing an errand with his father.

"What's up with you?" asked Mrs. Austin cheerfully.

"Well, you remember when I was asking you before the party about people who lived a hundred

☽

years ago, and you said there were letters and diaries to find out about them? Do you think there are any for the people who lived in that nursing home, like a hundred years ago?"

"What an interesting idea. There might well be. Why the nursing home?"

"No special reason. It's just so big and old, and I was wondering if it might have been entirely different a century ago."

"I've no doubt it was. Now luckily you have picked something I can help you with. A few years ago I was on a neighborhood commission to study traffic, when they were thinking of extending the subway out here. Part of our work was to look into the history of this neighborhood, and it so happens the Historical Society has a good-sized collection of materials from the old houses on these streets. It was fascinating work, though we could only skim the papers. So why don't you and I go over to the Society and ask to look up whatever might pertain to that house? Harry can come, too. A little dose of history would be good for him. They decided not to build the subway in the end."

"When can we go? Today?"

"That's awfully short notice. I'll call and find out the times when they're open—they don't have a full-time librarian, you see—and we'll go the very first chance we get."

Monday afternoon, after school, was the time they set. Winnie could hardly sit through school.

She thought she would never make it through math, and when Miss Bielin handed back the English class's compositions, Winnie put hers into her notebook without even remembering to read the comments.

Mrs. Austin was waiting on the front porch for Winnie at four o'clock. Harry sat on the top step, looking disgruntled.

Winnie had expected the museum to have marble columns and a couple of stone lions in front, but the Historical Society turned out to be two rooms over the Moloney Spa on Center Street. They climbed a steep flight of stairs, walked along a skinny, dim corridor to the back of the building, and there, at the end, were two rooms, painted gray, full of brown wooden desks and library tables and straight, hard chairs. Papers were piled everywhere like tilting haystacks. There were bookshelves, metal ones screwed together, up to the ceiling. A lady with tightly curled hair and glasses and a perfectly ironed white blouse looked up at them from a small table in one corner. That table was arranged with geometric precision: a telephone, a notepad, a large black typewriter, a jar of pencils.

"Can I help you?" the lady asked. "Oh, it's Mrs. Austin! I remember you from two years ago. And are these your children?"

"This one is," said Mrs. Austin, giving Harry a small push forward. "This is my son, Harry. Harry, this is Miss Sherbet. And this is our neighbor,

☽

Winnie Brown. We're here to do some research on the old Taylor house, if we may."

"Of course! It's so nice to see anyone, anyone at all!"

"It gets lonely up here, I expect," said Mrs. Austin.

"Not too many people are interested in local history," said Miss Sherbet. "They'd all rather watch *Miami Vice*. Did you happen to see it this week?"

"I'm afraid not," said Mrs. Austin. "We don't let Harry watch the violent programs."

"I don't blame you. I wouldn't allow a child to watch it, either. I wouldn't miss it myself, though. What do you watch?" she said to Winnie.

Winnie shrugged. *"Cosby* reruns."

"You can help yourself," said Miss Sherbet, turning back to the hills of paper and waving. "Do you know specifically what you want?"

"As I remember, there were a number of boxes from the Taylor house, some with letters, some with photographs."

"That's right. Twenty years ago, it must have been. Mrs. Lily Taylor Fields, over ninety when she died."

"I don't suppose you can put your hands right on those particular materials?"

Winnie barely heard them. Over ninety years old? Lily?

Miss Sherbet sat back and laughed. "That would be something—if I knew where everything was! You know, we were supposed to get a cataloguer to help us, but we never got the grant. You're welcome to look through our collection. Take your time. We were going to carry it all down to the basement to make room for some new records, but there's no hurry. The unbound things are mostly across the hall."

Mrs. Austin marched into the other gray room and surveyed the boxes ranged on the floor. Harry caught Winnie's eye and puffed out his cheeks and made noises, as if he were spitting tennis balls.

"Harry, stop that. If we can just find the right cartons . . ." Mrs. Austin opened the tops of some boxes. "This isn't it." Dust swirled in the air. Winnie sneezed. So this was research?

"Wait a second. Here we go." A stack of shoe boxes and cardboard cartons near the window had the last name *Taylor* scrawled on them in black marker. "Aha!" said Mrs. Austin with satisfaction, opening the top box. Winnie picked up a shoe box labeled "Bass Weejuns, 7½-B, $13.50" and looked beneath the lid. There on top was a fat envelope addressed to Mrs. Henry T. Fields from Mrs. William Sparrow. Winnie slid the folded pages out and opened them. "My dear Lily," the letter began. "What wonderful news. The birth of Daniel has given both of us great joy, and we are trying out our new titles—Great-aunt Harriet, Great-uncle Will." Winnie laid it aside and sifted through the other envelopes in the box—there were two to Mrs. Alfred Minot. So Violet had not been condemned to nonexistence for very long.

Winnie put the lid back on the box. She

☽

opened another carton and there were photographs, posed portraits in cardboard frames. One was of Lily as a young woman, maybe as old as eighteen, wearing a beautiful white dress and sitting on a bench, staring off into the distance beside a potted palm. There was another, not a portrait, taken on the back stoop: Thomas and Clara stood side by side, Thomas with his arm around Clara's shoulder, and both of them were smiling into the camera. Clara was wearing a wedding ring.

"Harry, look. Here's Thomas," Winnie said. Harry looked over her shoulder, and Mrs. Austin gave them a quizzical look. "Someone you know?" she said teasingly.

Another box held more letters, and a ledger book full of notes on the cost of repairs to the house, the purchase of a "motor car," the installation of a "water closet."

"Here's something odd—very odd." Mrs. Austin held up a sealed envelope. "I'm surprised no one ever opened this. It must have slipped out of sight when the family was cleaning out the house." On the envelope she handed to Winnie was written: "Do Not Open Until 1989 or After." The handwriting was large and round, and not particularly clear.

"It says don't open till this year," said Winnie.

"Yes, but people don't always follow directions like that. It looks rather like a child's prank. Do you want to be the one?"

Winnie unstuck the envelope—the glue was

dry and gave easily—and pulled out a folded bundle of paper. Across the top of the first page was written: "For the eyes of Winnie Brown and no one else, if she is alive." Winnie quickly shuffled to the last page, but she knew who the writer would be—Lily.

"What is it?" asked Mrs. Austin. "You have the strangest look on your face!"

"Look at this." Winnie showed her the page.

"Well, that's remarkable!" Mrs. Austin gave a short laugh. "There must have been some friend of this—who signed the letter?—this Lily—some friend with the same name as yours. It almost makes you think there was something more than coincidence working here. I suppose the explanation is that your name was not uncommon a hundred years ago. Winnie is a rather old-fashioned name now."

Winnie opened the letter to the first page and began to read.

August 27, 1889

Dear Winnie,

*I hope you read this letter someday,
because I don't think you'll come back here,
though I am still hoping I'll see you again
before the end of the summer. I was watching
from my window when you got Tab to go
into the maze, but Mrs. Minot crept out of
the house before I noticed, and even though I
made some noise, the way I told you I would,
she didn't look back once. She never came out*

☽

of the maze that night; she was nowhere in the house in the morning, and Clara couldn't find her anywhere. We were sitting in the kitchen together eating toast, when guess who walked into the kitchen? William! We both jumped up and began hugging him and crying and laughing and carrying on, and he wanted to know where Aunt Harriet was. So I told him she was gone on business but would be back in a few days. He said he was half starving to death, and Clara raced around to make him the biggest breakfast you have ever seen. Then, as we were talking, we saw Mrs. Minot come across the grass to the house. She didn't come through the kitchen but went around the other way, to her own apartment. She looked older, as if she had aged overnight.

The next day she told us that she and Alfred would be leaving Crescent Ridge in a few weeks and moving to the city, because Alfred had always wanted to own a store, and that's what they were going to do. She didn't care to stay at Crescent Ridge anymore. She said she knew Aunt Harriet would be upset because she had been there so long, but their minds were made up.

Later that same day William told me in confidence that he had seen you, and that you were safely home. He made me promise never to tell about his maze, and he said that in *any case, he had undone its powers. He had freed someone who was caught in it, and now no one could go through it ever again. Later I saw him sitting at Aunt Harriet's desk, though, and drawing a circular design with her pen, so I wonder if he means to keep himself from forgetting it. I promised I would never tell, because I do understand the danger, and I never will. But I can still write about it to you, because you already know; that's not breaking the promise.*

Two days later Aunt Harriet came back, and you should have seen her face when she drove up and William was standing on the steps! She was shocked that the Minots were leaving, but already Clara is in a better mood because of it (I think), and says her spells are letting up. She also turns pink right up to her forehead every time she sees Thomas. He likes to sit in the kitchen and watch her iron. Aunt Harriet and William have been spending hours in the library talking. I have a feeling Clara was right about them. What will Mama and Papa say? They'll have fits!

Mama and Papa's ship will have docked in New York by now, and they will come for me by the end of the week. I know they'll bring me lots of presents! I dread leaving Crescent Ridge, because I have a feeling it will never be so wonderful another time. Of course, I could be wrong.

☽

If you get this letter, Winnie, I beg
you—don't forget me! We were true and
good friends, even for a short time, a
hundred years ago.

> *Sincerely,*
> *Lily*
> *XOXOX*

P.S. I didn't know what to tell Aunt Harriet
about you, so I made something up. I said
that your uncle had come looking for you on
horseback, and that you had gone without
having time to write her a good-bye letter. I
assured her that you went entirely willingly
with your uncle, and that it was no hoax.

Winnie folded the pages of the letter together
slowly and looked up to see both Harry and Mrs.
Austin watching her. "I feel like this letter really
was written to me," she said carefully.

Mrs. Austin helped Winnie separate the boxes
of Taylor documents and stack them in a corner of
the room where Winnie could find them the next
time she came back. Miss Sherbet told her the
schedule. "Is it okay if I come by myself next
time?" asked Winnie. "Now that you know who I
am?"

"I'll be delighted to see you," said Miss Sherbet. "And bring your friend, too."

"I'm not sure I'll have time," said Harry.

"Well, then," said Miss Sherbet.

*　　*　　*

Winnie did go back on her own the next weekend, and spent hours reading through the Taylor letters while the radiators clanked and hissed. She had planned to return many more times, but she was too busy the next week, and the next. She saw Miss Sherbet at the bus stop one morning, and Miss Sherbet told her that they had had an awful misfortune: A pipe had burst in the basement and flooded all the documents stored there. Luckily, because Winnie had been reading it, the Taylor collection was still on the second floor, and so had escaped damage.

There was something else that Winnie still wanted to do, something she had thought of when she was at Crescent Ridge and afraid she might never get home. She wrote to her Grandmother and Grandfather Brown and told them she hoped she would see them sometime soon. It felt embarrassing to write the letter, because she couldn't think of a good excuse for seeing them, but she needn't have worried. Her grandmother wrote back and invited Winnie and her mother and Lew and Daisy to come for Thanksgiving dinner, and said that maybe Winnie could stay on for the rest of the weekend, so they could get to know her better.

Winnie's mother said that had been a thoughtful thing to do, and Lew said it was an excellent idea. Winnie wondered what it would be like this time, now that she was older and not as shy as she used to be. She knew she wouldn't be afraid to ask

☽

them about her father anymore; she could finally begin to find the part of her own past that was missing.

She hadn't been allowed to keep the letter from Lily, of course; she could never have convinced Miss Sherbet that it was really hers. But she thought of it as she reread her grandmother's note—how the two letters linked such distant parts of time, and she herself was the connection. She wondered what letters she would write someday to her own grandchildren.

Then she jumped up, put away the note, and grabbed her jacket from the back door hook. There was still time for a quick bike ride, and if she went up the street and dragged Harry away from the television now, they could make it twice around the pond before dark.

☼